"*Moon Shadow* is a gem of a [ ] only the enchantment of the night sky, but the magic of finding your own power and shining through life's challenges. Readers will fall in love with Lucia and cheer for her even after the last page is turned."
—KATE MESSNER, author of *The Seventh Wish*

"Lucia Frank is feeling abandoned, but she's afraid to tell anyone how she's feeling . . . until one magical moonlit night · when her voice is ignited. *Moon Shadow* is a tender story about being brave and finding the courage to speak up."
—SUZANNE SELFORS, author of the Imaginary Veterinary series

"*Moon Shadow* is amazing. . . . Kids are going to love it."
—COLBY SHARP, teacher, Nerdy Book Club cofounder, and cocreator of *The Yarn* podcast

"Must add to your middle-grade classroom. . . . Five stars; loved it so much."
—PERNILLE RIPP, teacher and founder of the Global Read Aloud

MOONshadow

ERIN DOWNING

ALADDIN

New York London Toronto Sydney New Delhi

ALADDIN

An imprint of Simon & Schuster Children's Publishing Division
1230 Avenue of the Americas, New York, New York 10020
First Aladdin paperback edition May 2018
Text copyright © 2017 by Erin Downing
Cover illustration copyright © 2017 by Julia Blattman
Also available in an Aladdin hardcover edition.
All rights reserved, including the right of reproduction in whole or in part in any form.
ALADDIN and related logo are registered trademarks of Simon & Schuster, Inc.
For information about special discounts for bulk purchases, please contact Simon & Schuster
Special Sales at 1-866-506-1949 or business@simonandschuster.com.
The Simon & Schuster Speakers Bureau can bring authors to your live event.
For more information or to book an event contact the Simon & Schuster Speakers
Bureau at 1-866-248-3049 or visit our website at www.simonspeakers.com.
Cover designed by Jessica Handelman
Interior designed by Greg Stadnyk
The text of this book was set in Garamond.
Manufactured in the United States of America 0418 OFF
2 4 6 8 10 9 7 5 3 1
The Library of Congress has cataloged the hardcover edition as follows:
Names: Downing, Erin, author.
Title: Moon shadow / by Erin Downing.
Description: First Aladdin hardcover edition. | New York : Aladdin, 2017. | Summary: "On the night of her thirteenth birthday, Lucia Frank's shadow half slips out and begins to act in ways that Lucia has always wanted but been afraid to do. Now Lucia is becoming the girl she's always wanted to be—fearless and assertive—but is there another cost to bear?"—Provided by publisher.
Identifiers: LCCN 2016047223 (print) | LCCN 2017021857 (eBook) |
ISBN 9781481475235 (eBook) | ISBN 9781481475211 (hc)
Subjects: | CYAC: Identity—Fiction. | Friendship—Fiction. | Dating (Social customs)—Fiction. |
High schools—Fiction. | Schools—Fiction. | Supernatural—Fiction. | BISAC: JUVENILE
FICTION / Social Issues / Friendship. | JUVENILE FICTION / Fantasy & Magic. | JUVENILE
FICTION / Legends, Myths, Fables / General.
Classification: LCC PZ7.D759273 (eBook) | LCC PZ7.D759273 Moo 2017 (print) |
DDC [Fic]—dc23
LC record available at https://lccn.loc.gov/2016047223
ISBN 9781481475228 (pbk)

For Greg,

boy next door turned husband extraordinaire

Unfortunately, there can be no doubt that man is, on the

whole, less good than he imagines himself or wants to be.

Everyone carries a shadow. . . .

—Carl Jung

We'll look at them together, then we'll take them apart. . . .

Multiply life by the power of two.

—Indigo Girls

CHAPTER ONE

Moon pies are obvious, right, Lucia?" Jonathan Bauer piled an armload of gooey, plastic-wrapped treats into our shopping cart. "Ooh! What about Nutty Bars?" He held a yellow box in front of my face, pleading with his huge, puppy-dog eyes.

I squinted back and asked, "How do Nutty Bars fit with an eclipse theme?"

"They're awesome?" Jonathan shrugged, then dumped them into the cart. "That must count for something."

Our friend Anji—short for Anjali—Mehta hollered from the next aisle over, "If we're going to ignore Lucia's food rules, then I vote for Doritos over Sun Chips!" I could hear her opening a bag of chips; the crunching echoed in the empty grocery store aisle. "It's your thirteenth birthday, Lu.

1

Shouldn't we celebrate in style? Sun Chips are the armpit of the chip section."

"Come on, you guys," I pleaded. "Sun Chips, moon pies, Starburst, star fruit . . . How lucky is it that star fruit is even in season somewhere in the world? Can we please stick with the theme?" I poked through our cart, admiring the small pile of outer-space-themed food we were buying for that night's lunar eclipse. The last total eclipse that had been visible in our little piece of the northeast was on the night I was born. Because of this birth connection, I'd been obsessed with eclipses my whole life, but I hadn't ever seen one live. "Besides, my dad only gave us twenty bucks. We can't afford much."

"Whoa," Jonathan said, holding up one hand. "Your dad gave you twenty bucks? Nice. Mine gave me nothing."

"Well, it is my birthday," I reminded him. "And I didn't want a cake."

Jonathan half smiled. "Even if it *were* my birthday, my dad wouldn't be handing over a twenty."

I didn't know what to say to that, so I pushed our cart around the corner and grabbed a chip from Anji's open bag of Doritos. Then I dropped it back in. I always felt guilty eating food I hadn't yet paid for. "Do you really want to ruin our eclipse feast with Doritos and Nutty Bars? I guarantee there will be other food at Velvet's party."

"Ugh. Don't remind me that we're going to *Velvet's party* to eat this stuff," Anji moaned. She rolled her eyes and put her hands on her hips, looking fierce in her green miniskirt and yellow tights. "Are you sure you want to go tonight? It feels wrong that this is how you want to celebrate *your* birthday."

"I'm sure," I said, even though I really wasn't.

Ever since first grade, Velvet Mills—self-appointed queen of the "Chosen Ones"—had hosted a huge annual party that every kid in our grade was invited to. In third grade she'd had a pool party at a fancy hotel. In fourth her parents rented out a whole bowling alley and let everyone order food off the menu. Last year, in sixth grade, Velvet's mom hired a party planner to turn their backyard into a full-on beach with sand and tiki lights and everything. There were hula dancers wiggling around, and this chubby guy hung out all night roasting a whole pig over a fire. Her parties were seriously over the top. Everyone talked about them for the rest of the year—which is exactly what Velvet wanted. She was the kind of person who lived to be loved and admired. Velvet was also one of the girls in our grade who nearly every other girl longed to be. Her dad was the chairman of Peep Records, she wore clothes you couldn't buy at a regular mall, and she oozed the kind of cool confidence I'll never have.

Until a few months ago there wouldn't have been any question about me going to my former-BFF's big fall bash. I used to do everything Velvet did, without a second thought. But that all changed last summer. Still, there were some parts of my old life I wasn't willing to let go. "We don't want to be the only seventh graders who don't show up. Trust me. Besides, Velvet's house has a killer roof deck where we'll have an amazing view of the eclipse." I folded my hands together and begged. "Pretty please . . . come with me?"

"You're telling me you want to go to Velvet's party because of a *roof deck*?" Anji sighed. She knew just enough about my history with Velvet that she couldn't stand my former best friend. I had only been hanging out with Anji and Jonathan for a month and a half—since the first week of seventh grade—but I had already discovered they were both unfailingly loyal. It's what I loved most about them. It's also what made them so different from Velvet. "Velvet doesn't deserve to have you there. You need to move on and get out of her shadow. Am I wrong?"

"No," I mumbled. "You're not wrong." But I was just being

agreeable. Even though Velvet had hurt me, deep down I didn't really want to believe that we would never be friends again or that my life would never go back to the way it once was. Velvet had knocked me down, but I guess a piece of me hoped that turning up at this party would be a good first step to show her that she couldn't *keep* me down. "But I still want to go. We can hide out on the roof deck with our eclipse treats."

Jonathan pulled a few random things out of our cart and stacked them on an empty store shelf. "Fine, no Nutty Bars," he muttered. "Meanie." He pushed his scruffy hair behind his ears and pouted, his head hanging heavy and low.

"I'm sorry!" My cheeks were flaming. I hated fighting, and I didn't want Jonathan or Anji to think I was a bully. Our friendship was still new enough that I often worried about ruining things. Reaching for the box of Nutty Bars, I said, "Get whatever you want. It's no biggie. And we don't have to go to Velvet's party if you don't want to. It was just an idea."

Anji tugged me toward the beverage coolers, immediately opening a Coke she pulled from the refrigerator. "Listen up, Ms. Frank: You are allowed to be bossy from time to time. *Especially* on your birthday. So no worries. This is your night." She grinned at me and said, "Just a hunch, but . . . I bet you made a list of every possible eclipse-themed food ages ago, didn't you? And now it's *killing* you that we're trying to stray from your plan. Jonathan was teasing."

"I know he's teasing." I forced a smile and nervously rubbed at the moonstone in my pocket, willing it to work its calming magic. The rock was a silly trinket my mom had tucked into my bassinet on the night I was born—an *amulet of protection*, she had reminded me a hundred times since then. I guess I'm supposed to feel connected to and calmed by the moonstone because I was born during an eclipse. I don't really buy it, but the stone is pretty—pure milky-white with a soft, greenish glow—and rubbing it usually does have a calming effect. "And no, I did *not* make a list of eclipse foods. This is spur of the moment, whimsical fun." I pointed into the cooler. "Look, Sunny Delight! Could there be a more perfect drink for tonight?" I hate Sunny Delight. It makes me gag. But it has the word "sun" in it, which made it perfect for the occasion.

As I set the Sunny D in the cart, Anji reached into my back pocket and pulled out the folded piece of paper I thought I'd so cleverly hidden. She read, "'Moon pies, Sunny Delight, Sun Chips, Starburst.' Hmm, that's funny. This looks like a list to me." She waved the paper around in the air.

"At least the star fruit was a late addition," I pointed out. "Karmic kismet."

"What's karmic kismet?" Jonathan asked.

"It sort of means fate delivered a happy little surprise," I told him. "A lucky accident. Finding a ripe star fruit is like the universe's reward for making me wait thirteen years to see my first eclipse. Since it's happening on my birthday, this whole night is karmic kismet, really."

"I'm beginning to figure out that *nothing* in your life is karmic kismet." Anji batted her eyelashes at me and rubbed one tiny hand through her short, spiky hair. "Do you realize you plan everything? Even bathroom breaks."

"I do not!" My face blazed with embarrassment. But I so *do*. Why risk it? Life is full of surprises, and few of them are good. I mean, math pop quizzes, getting your period, broken friendships, your parents' divorce . . . these are the types of things that just sort of sneak up on you. I'd prefer to live off a script, if that were an option. So I plan whatever I can, trying to keep control over as many pieces of my life as possible.

When I was little, my mom used to drag me around to visit her odd collection of friends who were astrologists and psychics and hypnotists and junk. She would lure me to their incense-laden houses with the promise of candy and cable TV, and watch hopefully as they predicted I'd have a long life and a happy family and all the other things a mom might wish for her daughter. Unfortunately, none of Mom's friends had ever told me exactly how my life would play out, and really, that would have been much more useful. I wish they could have outlined my life for me, put it into a tidy storyline that had moments of significance highlighted in green, so I'd know what to be prepared for.

Jonathan hopped up on the little bar on the back of the cart and twirled an invisible lasso, waiting for Anji to push him down the aisle. She giggled and gave him a shove. While Jonathan sailed toward the ice cream, Anji yelled back, "Second stall in the first floor bathroom, right after third and sixth period."

"Are you still talking about my bathroom schedule?" I cringed, my face getting even warmer. "And how do you even know that?"

Anji shrugged, as though it was normal that we were talking about my bathroom breaks. "I'm your friend. Friends keep tabs on one another. We share everything. I bet your body programs itself with the start of each school year, so you pee at ten fifty and two fifteen, even when you're home on the weekends. Tell me I'm right."

I grabbed the cart, pushing it and Jonathan toward the checkout lane. I was eager to get to Velvet's party and to get off this subject. I could see my sister, Romy, giving me the evil eye from out in the parking lot. She'd agreed to give us ten minutes to shop but promised she would leave us stranded if we were in the store any longer than that. When she first got her driver's license, Romy had promised to drive me everywhere as soon as she was allowed. She had talked about going to the movies, just the two of us, and driving us both to the pool in the summer. But ever since my parents' divorce, all her promises had been forgotten. After Mom left, Romy didn't like to do anything nice unless she was forced or bribed.

"Schedules are nice," I told Anji. "It's helpful to be predictable." Anji and Jonathan exchanged a look and laughed. Sometimes I still felt like an outsider with the two of them. They had gone to a different elementary school from me and had been best friends for years. I thanked my lucky stars that I had found them after Velvet had stranded me just before middle school began. Sometimes, though, our differences were super obvious. They were both so laid back. I was so *not*.

While I paid, Anji flipped through the magazine racks. "Check it out—an eclipse story! Landon and Langdon Louis are conjoined twins, connected at the head, who were magically separated during the last lunar eclipse." She gazed up from her trashy tabloid, eyebrows raised. "Cool."

"You *seem* smart, but . . . ," Jonathan started, trailing off. He pulled a dime from the depths of his pockets to round out my cash pool. "That's obviously made up—those aren't real names."

I laughed along, happy to have the conversation shift to something other than my bladder. While the checker bagged our stuff, I pulled another copy of the tabloid off the rack. The clerk was watching us closely, wise to the fact that we had no intention of buying the magazines. "Is it just the names that seem strange in that story?" I asked Jonathan. "You think the magical splitting of conjoined twins makes perfect sense?"

"Totally."

I glanced at the cover of the magazine and read another one of the subheadings: "'Vermont woman wishes for the return of her fiancé during Friday's lunar eclipse.' It looks like her fiancé mysteriously disappeared during the last eclipse. That's really sad."

"Well, she shouldn't have taken her eyes off him. The magic of the moon swept her true love away and left her alone. Or it could have been that the fiancé left her for someone else." Jonathan shrugged one shoulder. "Whatever. If it was the eclipse that made him disappear, I'm sure he'll reappear tonight—that's the way this kind of magic has to work, right? Otherwise they wouldn't have a story to print next month."

I nodded, despite the fact that stories like this gave me the heebie-jeebies. This was just the sort of thing I'd listened to my mom and her friends talk about when I was younger. Some people—my mom's kind of people—believed eclipses *were* magical. More than the sun, earth, and moon aligning and casting crazy shadows. For years I'd heard Mom's friends talking about legends and myths behind how and why the moon or sun got gobbled up by a dragon or an angry toad. Many cultures had their theories, but they all sounded silly to me.

Personally, I loved the way all the crazy stuff that happened up in the sky felt and looked like magic but had a solid foundation in science and planetary movement. Astronomical magic could be explained—unlike creepy-weird stuff like ghosts and shape-shifters and mind readers and other nonsense my mom bought into. I didn't believe in any of the made-up legends I'd heard Mom and her friends oohing and aahing about, but I did believe an eclipse would be beautiful. I couldn't wait to be tucked inside that fold between the moon and earth's shadow.

"Look at this," Jonathan said, paging through the magazine. "The Vermont lady is going to make a wish on the eclipse that her fiancé will come back. According to her and some space dude named Larry, wishing on an eclipse is like wishing on a star—but better. I think I'll try it."

I wouldn't mind a few wishes of my own coming true. As stupid as the idea sounded, I wondered if wishing on the eclipse was worth a shot. And did I get extra wishes because it was my birthday eclipse? That seemed only fair.

"It's seven," Anji said suddenly, dumping the tabloid on top of the candy display. "We need to move or we're not going to make it to Velvet's in time for the eclipse. Not that missing the party would be the *worst* thing in the world. . . ."

I stuffed the magazines back in the rack, taking one last look at the sad face of the woman with the lost fiancé. "I read online that they hire actors to pose for the pictures with those magazine stories," I said. "But how crazy would it be if something like this were real?"

Jonathan wiggled his fingers and *woo*ed like a ghost in a kid cartoon. Anji danced toward the sliding doors that led outside, singing, *"Once upon a time there was light in her life . . ."* She paused and turned back, pointing dramatically at me. *"Tonight is Lucia's night, for a total eclipse of the heart!"*

CHAPTER TWO

The first and only time I'd been inside Velvet's new house was almost two months ago, on the night of *her* thirteenth birthday. I could still remember a million little things about that night: the way my hair had cooperated (perfect curls), the exact color of my new shirt (sugar snap peas), and the way the air on Velvet's rooftop terrace had smelled like burning caramel and fresh paint.

One of her dad's washed-up boy bands serenaded Velvet, and Velvet sang "Big Girls Don't Cry." Even though she was turning thirteen, her mom—always super out of touch with what was age-appropriate—had bought Velvet a cake in the shape of Ariel from *The Little Mermaid*. My slice had Flounder on it, but the poor little fish's tail got chopped off when Velvet cut the cake.

I had just gotten back from spending my first post-divorce summer at my mom's new house in Sweden, so I hadn't seen Velvet since a few days after sixth grade had ended. I was so excited to catch up on everything that had happened while I was gone and plan for our first week of middle school. Velvet had hardly e-mailed or texted over the summer, but I knew she was always really busy with camps and stuff so it didn't surprise me. While I was gone, she and her parents had moved into a new house (a mansion, really), and I couldn't wait to help her figure out how to decorate her room.

For her big birthday she'd planned a slumber party for a group of girls she had dubbed the Chosen Ones. She had actually written *The Chosen Ones* (with a glittery little smiley face sticker in place of each of the *o*s), on the invitation. The name of the group had stuck after that night, minus one member: me.

When I arrived at her birthday party, I should have realized something was different. Velvet seemed extra loud and show-offy, and she didn't really pay much attention to me even though we hadn't seen each other in forever. There were a bunch of girls at the party I didn't know—girls who had gone to other elementary schools who would be in our new, bigger class at Hudson. I wasn't sure how Velvet had already gotten to know them, and I never got a chance to ask. A lot of girls who came to the party wore makeup, and almost all of them talked about boys. I felt like I'd blinked and woken up in someone else's life. I spent most of the night watching how the world I'd always known had changed while I was gone.

At first I blamed the weirdness between me and Velvet on a summer apart, thinking nothing important could have changed between friends in just a couple of months. But after my parents' divorce and a full summer away I was a little more cautious, less willing to trust people and the things they told me. When Velvet showed everyone around her bedroom later that night, I realized she had decorated it without me. Our bedrooms had always matched, but during the summer she had swapped her fleecy flower blanket for something ultra-chic and modern.

That night's birthday party had a murder mystery theme, where everyone was given a part to play and we had to hunt for clues to figure out who had supposedly done the crime. I was assigned the role of Clancy, a pipe-smoking, one-legged dude—the only male part in the game. Velvet informed me I had to hop around on one leg wearing a tweed vest that was rented from a costume shop. Velvet took the role of Tabitha, a beautiful model with a secret past. She got to wear a feather boa and a red leather miniskirt. All of the other girls were given equally glamorous parts and every one of them had a great time laughing at my costume. Eager to get the whole thing over with quickly, I solved the mystery in less than five minutes, thus ending the game. No one was happy with me for ruining their fun. It didn't take long after that—an evening of hushed whispers and secrets about get-togethers and conversations I hadn't been a part of—for me to realize I'd been left behind.

I tried to choke back the memory of that party when my sister pulled up in front of Velvet's massive house on the night of my own birthday. As soon as my friends and I stepped out of the car, I blurted out, "I heard one of Velvet's dad's new bands is playing tonight. We should be able to see their set from up on the roof. This is going to be fine, guys."

"Fine?" Anji prompted, raising her eyebrows at me. "Or fun?"

"Both?" I smiled widely to try to hide the anxiety that was threatening to strangle me before we even went inside. Anji made a gagging face. She refused to hide her dislike of Velvet and her Chosen Ones.

There was a note on the outside of the enormous door that said *Come on in!*, so I pushed it open and stepped inside. My friends' eyes grew wide as they took in the expansive foyer and massive marble lion that stood in the middle of the front hall. The lion had a pom-pom in Hudson Middle School colors atop its head.

"Tacky," Jonathan muttered. I swatted his arm, even though I was sure no one could hear him over the noise of the party. "What? It's a lion wearing a plastic wig."

Anji stopped us just inside the door and pulled a tiny mirror out of her bag. She dabbed a silvery powder over her lips, then slathered on goopy gloss that shimmered in the low lights of Velvet's foyer. "Your lips look like a disco ball," I told her, laughing.

"That was the plan." When she smiled at me, Anji had to hold her lips at a weird angle so the glittery sheen wouldn't smudge onto her teeth. Anji loved to stand out. The funny thing is, her parents are super strict about stuff like makeup, so Anji has to wait until she leaves her house to put on her "face." I wish I had the guts to rebel the way she does.

"My jeans are stuck to my thighs," I said quietly as we wandered through the lower level of Velvet's house. It was unseasonably warm for October in New York, but I was also feeling really nervous. "Is anyone else hot? I'm sweating like a ninja."

"I don't think ninjas sweat," Jonathan whispered back. "That's part of the reason they're so sneaky."

Eventually we made it to the kitchen. I scanned the room and noticed that Velvet's parents were nowhere to be seen, thank goodness. I hadn't seen Velvet's mom since that end-of-summer birthday sleepover, when I'd called my dad to come and get me in the middle of the night. Mr. Mills's absence was less surprising. In all the years I'd known Velvet, I'd only seen him at home once or twice. Unlike my dad, who—except for going to work—was literally *always* home lately.

As in other years, Velvet's parents had hired people to manage the party for them. So a bunch of random adults were bustling around with snack bowls, two-liter bottles of soda, and cleaning supplies. "Do we need to check in or something, or can we just sneak up to the roof?" Jonathan grumbled.

Jonathan and I were both uncomfortable in crowds of strangers. There were at least a hundred people at the party, and a quick glance around the kitchen told me I didn't know a lot of them. I waved to a couple of people I knew from elementary school. There were a few other kids I had classes with or had passed in the halls at school. But a lot of the crowd surrounding us was made up of total strangers. I wondered how many of these kids were actually friends with Velvet . . . and how many had just come for free snacks and the band. Jonathan scanned the crowd on the sloping lawn outside and groaned, "Can we *please* hit the roof deck now? I'm starving for Starburst."

Just as he said that, Velvet came traipsing into the kitchen. Velvet's perfume—when had she started wearing perfume?—filled the room with a grapefruity aura. Her smooth, bobbed black hair fell across her face at an angle, and I instinctively reached up to push my own overly long bangs away from my eyes. "Oh, *hi*, Lucia," Velvet purred. "I'm surprised you came. And you brought . . . them." She didn't even look at Jonathan and Anji when she said the word "them." "The lovebirds, right?"

I caught Anji and Jonathan exchanging eye-rolls. They were good friends, nothing more, and I knew they both found it annoying when people asked if they were a couple or something. I wanted to tell Velvet to just butt out, but Anji beat me to it. "Nope," she muttered, gritting her teeth. "Just friends."

Under her breath, I heard her say, "But I don't think you get the meaning of that word."

I glanced quickly at Velvet, wondering if she'd heard what Anji had said. It seemed like she hadn't. But Velvet caught my eye and said, "Obviously it's fine that you *all* came. Anyone was invited. This party isn't just for friends."

I tried not to let her words get to me. Tried not to feel sad that I was no longer a part of her circle. The truth, though, is that I *do* care. Even though I've always pretended to be happy in the outer orbit—first as one of Velvet's followers and now as an unpopular nobody—there have been many times I've wished I were a different kind of person: the kind of girl who speaks her mind, dances at school dances, auditions for school plays. But wishing is as far as I'll ever get. Because the second any kind of spotlight shines on me, I clam up like some sort of fool and act like a puppet waiting for stage directions. That's one of the things I most enjoyed about being friends with Velvet. She let me hang out in her shadow, occasionally tugging my strings and telling me what to do. My very own Geppetto.

A moment later the French doors leading out to the patio opened, and Will Barton stepped inside. He touched Velvet's arm, and I looked at the floor, trying to blend into the tiled wall behind me. "Hey, Velvet—do you have any chocolate bars? We want to make s'mores."

"If we don't, we can send someone out to get some," Velvet said. I glanced up just in time to see her touch Will's arm in a flirty way. She giggled and added, "But only for you."

I kind of wanted to throw up. I *hated* seeing Will and Velvet together. Like most of the other couples in our grade, Velvet and Will mostly ignored each other during the school day. But outside school, I guess things were different. She was touching his arm! *Yuck.* As far as I was concerned, Will and Velvet made a terrible couple. Unfortunately, I had made the mistake of telling Velvet that when they first got together.

Looking back on Velvet's birthday party, I wish I could say it was something silly, like refusing to ice Courtney Tambor's bra, that froze me out of Velvet's circle. But it wasn't. It was because of how I had reacted when I found out she and Will had started hanging out over the summer. Will, my neighbor and forever friend, and Velvet, the girl I'd always considered my other best friend. Before last summer their only connection had been me.

Even though I'd never liked Will as anything more than a friend, I had totally freaked out when Velvet cruelly announced that the two of them were now *a thing*. Because when she told me, Velvet also made it very clear that I would no longer be allowed to hang out with Will. He was *hers* now. And Velvet always got her way. Losing both Will *and* Velvet—on top of everything that had already happened with my parents' divorce—was enough to crack me. Velvet didn't like to see weakness. When I fell apart, my supposed best friend ditched me like a broken toy.

Every time I saw the two of them together after that, it stung.

"Oh, hey, Lucia," Will said awkwardly, untangling himself from Velvet's arm to grab a soda from the fridge. "Happy birthday."

"Thanks." I shifted my gaze back to the floor.

"Oh right!" Velvet cooed, touching Will's arm again. The gesture was like her annoying little birthday gift for me. "It's today, isn't it? I totally forgot."

Anji snorted, and I shot her a warning look. She clenched her jaw and folded her arms over her chest. I know she wished I would stick up for myself more around Velvet. *I* wished I could too, but I'm just not that kind of person.

"I'm glad you came tonight," Will said, smiling. "I was starting to think I might have to watch your birthday eclipse without you." He nudged me, a friendly gesture, and I stepped away. I didn't want Velvet to think I was trying to steal him from her or something.

"We brought fun snacks," I mumbled. "Anji and Jonathan and I were hoping to watch the eclipse up on the roof." This was the most I'd said to Will in months. I glanced at Velvet and added, "If that's okay?"

"Theme food?" Will asked, his eyes lighting up. He flashed his goofy, gap-toothed smile. When he pushed his hair off his face, I could see the scar above his eyebrow from that time he'd fallen out of his backyard tree house. I remembered that fall like it was yesterday and also the awful couple of days that followed when he wasn't around for me to hang out with. Funny how a few days had felt like an eternity back then.

Now it had been four months since Will and I had talked— really talked, the way we used to. I didn't think a friendship like mine and Will's could end so suddenly. But I guess if I'd learned anything in the past few months, it was that any relationship could crumble without warning. There are no guarantees. Stuff happens, and then your happy old life gets kicked and trampled and left for dead in a ditch.

Will reached out to grab the bag of food. "Lemme see what you got."

Velvet gave me a pitying look before cooing, "If you want to hide away upstairs, Lucia, be my guest. But come on, Will. Are you really going to miss my party to watch the moon move? We can hang out by the bonfire before the band starts. I'll roast you a marshmallow."

"I really want to see the eclipse," Will said plainly.

"But you can stay down here to watch it. With everyone else." Velvet was smiling, but her body was tense. I knew that tone of voice well. Her bossiness had always worked on me. Eager to avoid arguments, I had always done whatever she said when she talked to me like that. I always got stuck being Ken when we were playing with Barbies. Her American Girl doll always got to use my doll's crutches when she came over to my house. She always decided what our first-day-of-school outfits were going to be, and I willingly followed her lead. Letting her have her way was easier than listening to her whine later.

Will sighed, and I thought he was going to cave. But then he turned away from Velvet and started toward the stairs. He called out over his shoulder, "Lucia has been waiting to see an eclipse forever, and I want to watch it with her. Later, V." He gave Velvet a flip little wave. My friends and I followed him through the foyer and up the plush staircase. Anji nudged me and I shrugged. I had no idea what was going on between Will and Velvet, but as I thought about how Will had blown her off, a teeny, tiny smile tugged at the corner of my mouth. Then I erased it quick before anyone could see.

CHAPTER THREE

nji, Jonathan, and I trailed behind Will up the stairs. Despite the enormity of Velvet's house, the dark color on the walls made everything feel tight and twisting, like a maze. Halfway down one long hall, Will opened a door and led us up another staircase.

The rooftop terrace was decked out like one of the outdoor pages in a home design catalog. It hadn't looked like this on the night of Velvet's birthday party, so I was momentarily disoriented. There were these cute little cabanas in every corner. The middle of the patio was outfitted with a neat line of padded lounge chairs, each with an amazing view of the entire night sky. The moon glowed overhead, full and butter yellow. The walls around the patio were low, so we could see the sky stretching out to the edge of our town on three sides. If we were a little higher up, we might have been able to see the New York City skyline glimmering way off in the distance. The fourth side of the patio was walled off by darkened glass with a door that led into a study of some kind. "What's this?" Anji asked, reaching for the doorknob.

"Don't go in there," Will said so abruptly that Anji pulled her hand away. "It's Velvet's dad's studio, and he's not big on people going in there. I've only been in a few times myself." I cringed. He spoke about Velvet's house and parents like he was part of their family or something now. It still freaked me out to think about the two of them hanging out together the way they each used to hang out with me.

After Will and I settled into chairs on the terrace, I spilled open our bag of snacks. Anji and Jonathan grabbed a bunch of Starburst, then walked to the edge of the roof and looked down at the people gathered below. I could hear them making up stories about our classmates, creating fake little dramas to amuse each other.

"I had a feeling you'd do something like this," Will said, gesturing to the outer-space-themed food. "It's totally you."

"It's silly," I said, finally starting to relax. "But I knew I

28

had to do something fun for my birthday eclipse. My mom will be disappointed I didn't find some sort of moon worship circle to celebrate with. I guess I should be dancing and howling or something, to really honor such an important day."

Will raked a hand through his hair and rubbed his tongue over the gap in his front teeth. "You are the Moon Child," he said seriously. "There are certain duties that go along with such an important title." We both laughed.

"I can't believe you remember that," I said, shaking my head. Mom and her friend Suze had called me Moon Child until I was old enough to make them stop. Because of the eclipse on my birth night, they felt the moon had somehow claimed me as one of her own. *Her.* Who knew the moon was female?

"Remember what we called me?" Will asked.

Of course I remembered. I remembered everything about Will—because whenever I hung out with him in the safety of our connected backyards, I had always felt comfortable being my real self. In my family, I was the uncomplaining kid who helped keep the peace. Hidden under Velvet's wing, I was a follower. At school, I was invisible. But with Will it was different.

29

When we were little, Will and I spent summer days digging for worms under the giant garden rocks, testing the volcanic power of Diet Coke mixed with mint Mentos, or hiding out in our tree fort watching the stars and their constellations slowly appear as the day sky turned to dusk and then dark. Then we would go to his house, and his mom would stuff us with homemade cookies, these delicious mint chocolate sandwich cookies that I'd never been able to replicate on my own (I'd tried and given my whole family terrible gas). They were really, really good cookies, and it made me sort of sick to think that Velvet could eat those cookies whenever she wanted.

"You don't remember!" Will said accusingly after I'd been silent for a few seconds. "Ouch."

"The Full Mooner," I said. "You called yourself the Full Mooner. Don't bring me into this. I had nothing to do with that stupid name!"

He giggled—really, truly giggled, like he had when he was seven—which made me start giggling too. When Will snorted, Anji turned and raised her eyebrows at us. "That's such a horrible name," I gasped. "Really, really brutal."

"Hey, don't knock it." He relaxed back into his lounge chair, and we both stared up at the sky. Before long, the silence hung heavy between us again. I hated that I could no longer just *be* around him. It never used to be like this. As kids we spent hours together every day. Every second I wasn't with Velvet, I was with Will. Last spring he was the one who helped me survive the days of watching my parents separate their lives, putting this and that into boxes of his and hers. He had listened to all my dumb complaints and helped me remember to laugh when all I wanted to do was cry. He had been a best friend in the truest sense of the word.

I squeezed my eyes closed, because suddenly the only thing I could think about was the fact that Will and I had kissed. It was right after sixth grade ended, the afternoon before I left for Sweden to spend the summer with my mom. Sometime near the end of fifth grade, Will and I had been joking around one day and agreed that if neither of us had kissed anyone before we started middle school, we should get our first kiss out of the way with each other.

When it happened, the kiss was super awkward, and we both laughed about it as soon as it was over. We just weren't meant to be boyfriend-girlfriend. I don't know why I thought kissing him would be a good idea. It was kind of wet and slimy, and afterward I felt the tiniest bit uncomfortable around him for the first time ever.

Later that night, after she'd begged me to tell her why I was acting so weird, I'd told Velvet everything. I told her about the kiss and wondered aloud if things were going to be different between Will and me when I got back from Sweden. I asked her, "Do you think Will likes me . . . *like that*?" I didn't like him as anything more than a friend, so I hoped the answer was no—but I didn't tell Velvet that. Still, Will was one of my best friends, and I didn't want to ruin anything. I was pretty sure he felt the same.

Velvet had laughed in a mean way and said, "It sounds like it was a disaster. Maybe you need kissing lessons."

"It wasn't awful," I argued, my face red. "But we're just better friends than *more than friends*. At least, I think we are?"

That's when Velvet had said suddenly, "Jasmine Hendricks told me she heard Will likes *me*." She pushed her hair behind her ear and added, "Maybe he was just using you as practice for kissing me."

I stared at her. "Are you serious?"

Velvet shrugged.

"You would make a terrible couple!" I said before hastily

covering my mouth. But it was true. Velvet and Will would be awful together. They had nothing in common—other than both being friends with me.

"How do you know?" Velvet asked in a snappy tone.

"Because I just do," I said softly. "You're both great, but—"

"But what?" Velvet demanded. Then she smirked at me and said, "Well, I guess we'll have to see what happens."

I didn't know what she meant then, but I soon found out. I guess she'd taken what I'd said as a challenge or something. Or maybe she was jealous that I had kissed someone before she had. Velvet had always been first to do everything, and she didn't like when I had something she didn't. Velvet had never really paid much attention to Will before that day. The two of them were separate, opposite parts of my life. But suddenly she seemed interested in him as something more than the "obnoxious guy" who lived next door to me.

A few months later, on the night of Velvet's awful birthday party, twenty girls watched as Velvet announced to me that Will was her boyfriend now—and so that made him off-limits to any other girls, especially me. "I'm sorry if you're upset that he likes me more, Lucia. Just so you know, I told him how you feel about him and he laughed."

"How I feel about him?" I whispered. I *felt* that he was my friend—nothing more. "What did you say?"

"I told him you'd told me all about the kiss," she said sweetly. "And I also told him how much you'd been looking forward to kissing him again when you got home from Sweden." A few of the other girls at the party laughed. One girl I had just met that night, Ceriah, chewed her lip and gave me a look that told me she felt sorry for me. Velvet shrugged and said, "I guess this means he likes me more than he ever liked you."

Without warning, tears welled up in my eyes. That's when I realized I should never have told her about the kiss. I should have kept it a secret between Will and me, and I definitely never should have announced to Velvet that I thought they would make a terrible couple. Her talking to Will about that stupid kiss was almost as bad as if she'd written a note on purple-lined stationery, telling him to check a box, yes or no, to say if he liked me back.

I had spent the whole summer hoping Will and I would be able to go back to the way things used to be, before the dumb old kiss. But instead, Velvet had taken control, as she always did, and ruined everything. How could I face him now that he thought I liked him as more than a friend? And she'd told him I had been hoping to kiss him again! That was so far from the truth.

"I've always liked Will—you know that," Velvet said with a casual shrug as she stared straight into my eyes. I knew she was lying. She had taken him just to prove that she could have anything she wanted. Then she tilted her head, smiled a pitying smile, and said, "I'm sorry about your crush, Lucia. I'm sure you'll get over it. And I really am sorry if you're disappointed he picked me over you, but he told me it was never like that with you. He's never really liked you. He just feels bad for you because of everything with your parents."

I was totally humiliated. Nothing had been the same between any of us since. I guess Will was uncomfortable about the whole situation too, since he had mostly avoided me once school had started. We never met up in his tree house anymore, and we didn't even share a ride to school. Everything had changed because of that kiss and because of Velvet. I wasn't heartbroken that I'd lost Will as a possible boyfriend, but I was devastated that I'd lost him as a friend.

When I opened my eyes again, Will was looking at me. He couldn't have known I was thinking about the kiss, but even still, I blushed. Anji and Jonathan plunked down on lounge chairs next to us then. Will kept looking at me with this weird expression that made me feel like he had something to say. But I stared down at my lap, eager to avoid his eyes. It was hard for me to read him.

He'd changed.

I'd changed.

We'd changed.

I was so busy trying to stay occupied and contribute to the conversation without looking at Will that I mindlessly downed an entire bottle of root beer in less than half an hour. I suddenly and desperately needed to pee. It was after ten, and I had exactly six minutes before the total eclipse began, so I excused myself and ran down the stairs. I got lost several times trying to locate one of the many powder rooms. Though the main floor of Velvet's house was crowded and lively, the upstairs was empty and still, and it gave me the willies.

By the time I'd found a bathroom, I had no idea where I was anymore. I realized I should have left a trail of Starburst to help me find my way back to my friends. I hustled through the corridors. There were closed doors everywhere, leading to who knows where. I was certain I'd be lost for all eternity in Velvet Mills's mansion.

As I slipped through the halls, I heard Velvet talking to someone in her bedroom at the end of the hallway. I was tempted to sneak down the hall for just a minute, curious to hear what Velvet had to say. But ultimately, the fear of getting caught or missing the eclipse made me hustle in the other direction.

I opened a door that looked vaguely familiar and found a set of stairs that led upward—to the roof, I hoped. I climbed quickly and pushed open the door at the top. I was on a roof, but nothing looked familiar. Only two chairs, no cabanas, no friends. I'd somehow led myself to a deserted garden terrace that smelled of fresh lavender. It was dark and deserted, nothing like the rooftop deck where my friends were waiting.

My body tensed with the realization that I was alone. But then I heard Anji's laughter from somewhere nearby and relaxed. I called out to my friends, but the band Velvet's dad had hired for the party began to play a loud song down in the yard, and I knew no one could hear me. I noticed a wall of glass on the far end of my terrace that looked very much like the wall on the other side of the roof. The rooftop must be split into halves divided by Velvet's dad's office, I realized, and I had simply managed to find my way out to the *other* side of the roof.

I glanced up. There was only the tiniest sliver of bright moon left. If I ran back down the stairs and tried to find my way up again, I would miss the magical first moment of total eclipse. After a brief internal debate about politeness and appropriateness, I decided to try to cut through Velvet's dad's studio. It was the easiest and quickest way back to my friends.

I hustled across the expansive rooftop. The band transitioned into a bass solo in the yard below, and in that moment of quietness the crinkle of moon pie wrappers echoed through the still night. To keep myself from getting any more spooked, I rubbed my moonstone and thought about all the things I would wish for during my birthday eclipse:

I wished for Will—that he and I could go back to being friends like we were before.

I wished for guts—to let both Velvet and my mom know how much they'd hurt me this year.

I wished for confidence—to speak the truth, rather than kicking my anger deep down to fester and rot and boil inside.

I wished for bravery—that I might find my moment to step out of the shadows to shine.

If the first star of the night were worth one wish—*Star light, star bright / First star I see tonight*—how many would wishing on the eclipse get me? How many wishes might it take to change my life?

A cool blast of night air blew over the roof wall. Just as the moon took its last timid step into the full, round shadow of the earth, I heard the tentative crunch of a footstep on the terrace behind me. I was momentarily frozen with all those unspoken wishes trapped on my tongue. Suddenly, and without warning, I felt myself crumple to the ground.

OUT OF THE SHADOWS

The girl stirred, cracking her eyes open under the inky redness of the eclipsed and hidden moon. She stood up and peered over the wall as the pounding bass of the band echoed around her. Smoke from the bonfire filled the air with a dusty haze that made the shadowed moon overhead look even more magical. Her lips parted, and when she sucked in, she could taste the tangy sweet flavor of a red Starburst on her tongue.

"Hey." The boy's voice startled her, but when she turned, she found she wasn't surprised to see him there. He smiled before stepping out of the shadows to join her at the edge of the roof. He glanced at her sideways and said, "I've been looking for you—you didn't come back. Is everything okay?" Concern passed across his face, and she realized there were secrets hidden deep within his words. Secrets she wanted to uncover. "Listen, I—"

"I think we need to talk," she blurted out. It was time to take back what she'd lost. If she never said anything, he would be gone from her life forever. She wasn't willing to let that happen. "Really talk. About everything. I've missed you. I wish we were still friends like before."

"Yeah," he said, obviously relieved. "Me too. Want to meet up tomorrow night? The old spot?"

"Of course." She squinted at him. Then she added, "She was wrong, you know. What she told you about me and you and the kiss. It was just a stupid mistake, and it never should have turned into such a big deal." The girl shrugged. "I should have said something sooner. Can we pretend none of it ever happened? Go back to the way things were before?"

"For sure." He nodded and pulled her close for a hug. "Friends always."

CHAPTER FOUR

rubbed my head as I looked up into the bright, moonlit sky. The total eclipse was obviously over. I was sitting on one of the lounge chairs on the deserted terrace, cuddled up inside a cashmere throw. I could smell the thick, smoky air from the bonfire wafting up from the yard below and the band was still playing. Confused, I shook my head to clear it and looked around. I dug my fingers into my hair—I couldn't feel a goose egg or even any pain. But I was pretty sure something on the outskirts of normal had just happened. I had been walking across the terrace, I'd heard a footstep, and then—*plop*.

Taking a deep breath, I reached inside my pocket and rubbed a finger over my moonstone. It was cool and smooth and instantly made me feel more at ease. When I wrapped the stone inside my palm, the outline of a dream flickered through my head. Something about Will and me and the eclipsed moon and . . . that was it. As quickly as the scene appeared in my head, it was gone again. It felt a little like déjà vu, but not. A memory and a dream and a wish, all bundled up together into one strange little package.

"You're pitiful." Suddenly Velvet appeared beside me, her voice dripping hate like icicles. "Seriously, why don't you just let him go?" Velvet didn't let her true colors show that often, but when she did, they shone bright. "What are you doing up here, Lucia? This is my parents' private terrace."

"I got lost," I said, vaguely recalling what had happened. I'd gone up a set of stairs, ended up on the wrong part of the roof, and fainted or something, totally missing my birthday eclipse.

"You got *lost*? Or you were sneaking around?" Her voice escalated, and her hands clenched into fists. "You need to learn to stay away from things that aren't yours."

"What are you talking about?" I asked. Did she think I was trying to steal something? Whatever. I had much more important things to deal with at the moment, such as: What on earth had just happened to me? The total eclipse was supposed to have lasted around an hour—was I out for that long? I quickly glanced down at my phone. Yep, fifty-seven minutes. If this were a TV show, losing an hour of my life might not seem that odd. In the grand scheme of *my* life, however, a misplaced hour was somewhat unsettling.

"Where. Is. Will?" Velvet said, glaring at me.

"I don't know where Will is, Velvet. He's obviously not with me." *He's your boyfriend,* I wanted to remind her. *Maybe you should keep a closer eye on him or you'll lose him the way I did.* Though my mouth opened as if to speak, I couldn't—wouldn't—say it out loud.

"He was up here with you," she spat. Her teeth were biting down on her lip so hard that her whole lower lip went white. "I *saw* you."

Velvet knew Will had come up to the roof with Anji, Jonathan, and me—so why was she acting so weird? Had she seen something that made her suspicious? I glanced around, searching for hidden cameras. She would do that sort of thing. Velvet was a paranoid type of person. Before I could stop myself, I blurted out, "Stop acting jealous and crazy, Velvet. If I want to talk to Will, I'll talk to him. You have no right to boss me around anymore."

Velvet reacted like I'd slapped her. I realized this was the first time I'd ever talked back to her like that, and I relished how good it felt. She narrowed her eyes and said, "I could make your life much worse than it already is, you know."

"Seriously, Velvet, why are you being like this?" I asked. "Why do you need to be so mean?" Velvet scowled at me, and I immediately felt guilty. I muttered, "Sorry. I'm just having a really weird night."

She stared at me for a moment longer, then turned away. She was obviously upset. About what, I had no idea.

"Are you crying?" I asked, shocked.

"Ugh," she blurted out, reeling around to face me with a sneer. "Obviously I'm not *crying*."

But I knew her well enough to feel pretty certain she had been close. I had only seen Velvet cry once before. It had been a few years ago, but I'd never forgotten, because it was so unusual. Velvet had never been the kind of kid who was coddled and nurtured and wrapped in blankets when she tripped or felt sad. So she had learned to cope, to deal.

But one day, when we were ten, Velvet had cracked, and I'd seen something inside her that scared me a little. We'd been sitting at the pool, dangling our legs in the water, and I'd noticed that Velvet had shaved her legs. Her leg brushed against mine in the water, and it felt slimy and naked, strange next to my own. It suddenly seemed that Velvet was all grown up, and I was still a little girl, my legs soft with downy fur. It was strange how something as simple as shaved legs could set two girls apart, but I remember that was the day I'd realized just how different we were. How different our lives were. My mom would never let me near a razor, would never let me shave my legs, and I'd said as much to Velvet.

She'd looked at me, then down at her own legs, and inexplicably started to cry.

"What's wrong?" I'd pleaded, scared that my strong, confident friend was hurting. "Did you cut yourself?"

"No," she'd said harshly, giving me that look that reminded me how stupid I could be around her. "I didn't *cut myself*."

I'd ducked my head, embarrassed that, once again, I just didn't get it. I'd never seemed to get it with Velvet.

"Did I ever tell you I was an accident?" she had said finally, kicking her legs in the water. Her purple-nailed toes floated up toward the surface, and I could see tiny yellow flowers painted on each one. The one on her big left toe was chipping. "My parents never even wanted me."

"That's not true," I insisted, reaching for her hand. "You're perfect. Of course they want you."

Velvet shrugged but let me take her hand. "I heard them fighting. My mom told my dad that having a kid was a mistake. She said everything would be different if she had never gotten pregnant."

"But she did get pregnant. With you," I said, not understanding how anyone could regret someone as beautiful as Velvet. "And your life is so perfect. They give you everything."

Velvet choked on a laugh through her tears. "They give me everything, but they don't even notice I'm here," she said. "Your mom would know if you shaved your legs. My parents wouldn't even notice if I was gone."

"That's not true," I insisted. We both knew she was just being dramatic. "They love you." She ignored me and dove into the water. She never said anything about it again—and I never asked.

"Velvet," I said now, standing up to touch her shoulder as we lingered there together on the roof. "Are you okay?"

She shoved my hand away and snapped, *"Don't touch me!"* Then she was gone. I waited a few minutes to give her some space, and then followed her down the little rooftop stairs. I easily found my way outside. The party was still in full swing, and most of our class had spilled out across the enormous lawn. When I sat down on a bench at the edge of the party, I read through several text messages from Anji and Jonathan, asking me where I was. I texted them back, letting them know I was waiting outside, ready to get out of there. Then I texted my sister and asked her to pick us up. I hoped she would hurry.

As I wandered through the yard, no one noticed me. The band had finally wrapped up and gone. Some kids had already been picked up by their parents, but dozens remained—sprinkled in clusters of friends around the lawn and down by the creek at the bottom of Velvet's yard. Will and some of his friends were poking at the bonfire, attacking one another with charred, sticky marshmallows. Velvet held court among the girls, who tried to flirt and capture the boys' attention.

From afar, I could hear some of them talking about meeting up for a bonfire near the river the next night. Everyone planned to gather at Jake Sumter's house. His sprawling backyard butted up to the river, and they could cross to the sheltered area under the footbridge. I was instantly jealous. Will's friends and Velvet's friends had merged over the summer while I was gone. I thought about how I used to be part of that group. But I was only included because I was with Velvet. Without her, I had discovered, I was no longer welcome. I left the backyard. I didn't want to know what I was missing. There were many times I'd wondered: If I had Velvet's confidence and power, how would my life be different?

While we sat out front, waiting for my sister to pick us up, Anji and Jonathan quizzed me about where I'd been. "We were worried about you," Jonathan said. "You never came back. You're the only person we really know at this party, and when you didn't come back—" He shook his head. "I mean, what the heck, Lucia? Where did you go?"

"We thought maybe you had become one of Velvet's minions again. Ditched us," Anji said. She looked over at me, beseeching. "You didn't, did you?"

"No." I forced a laugh. Because she'd told me, I knew Anji fretted about what people thought of her much more than she let on. For some reason Anji worried that I was going to abandon them for Velvet. I hadn't ever told her and Jonathan the specifics of what had happened between me and Velvet and Will. It wasn't like they could change anything, so what was the point of complaining about it? But I knew I'd never do to them what Velvet had done to me. "Definitely not that."

I wondered how much I should tell my friends about my strange night and the lost hour. I wasn't hurt, just a little scared and weirded-out. What if I told them and they thought I was crazy? "I guess I just somehow ended up on a different part of Velvet's roof," I said lightly, ignoring the voice in my head that told me I should confess everything. "I got lost. Then I didn't want to miss the eclipse, so I stayed there until it was over. I'm sorry."

"Was Will with you?" Anji asked. "Or did Velvet tug his leash and finally get him to heel by her side?"

I looked at her. "Will wasn't with you during the eclipse? Where'd he go?"

"Beats me," Anji said. "He left to look for you after you didn't come back."

I let that sink in. If Will wasn't with Anji and Jonathan, where was he? I thought back to my conversation with Velvet, then tugged at the memory of the strange dream I'd had while I was asleep or knocked out or whatever. But I couldn't extract any more details.

"The eclipse was crazy cool," Jonathan said. "So orange!"

I nodded vaguely. Even though I hadn't seen the total eclipse,

I knew that some things about that night had definitely been crazy. I was disappointed that I'd somehow missed seeing my own birthday eclipse, but my big concern was how a whole hour of my life seemed to have evaporated into thin air.

What was going on?

CHAPTER FIVE

When I woke up late the next morning, I found my dad in the middle of our living room, his leg twisted into Tree Pose. *"Namaste,"* he called to me over the sound of rolling waves. When he did his yoga, Dad listened to *Ocean Wanderings* or *Natural Morning*. I was glad it was waves that day, since *Natural Morning* sounded a little like animals near death.

"Namaste." I lifted a hand and saluted while pouring myself a bowl of very unnatural Lucky Charms. "And top o' the mornin' to you!"

"This really is the last time I'm buying that crap, Lucia." My dad said this halfheartedly. He loved sugar cereal too.

"Bite?" I offered, wandering over to curl up on the couch next to my dad's yoga mat. He was down on all fours but opened his mouth and happily accepted a spoonful of sugary marshmallows. "That's a priceless image, Dad. How often do you see a combination of Cat/Cow and Lucky Charms?"

"Don't tell anyone, okay?"

"You got it," I promised. My dad was the biggest faker when it came to natural and homeopathic stuff like yoga and healthy eating. He was a closet McDonald's junkie and had used his gym membership maybe three times in the last year. The yoga thing was relatively new—I was pretty sure he'd become Captain Om only because I'd told him about the "core, mind, and body" retreats Mom and her new girlfriend, Johanna, had tried to drag me to this summer in Sweden. Even though he would never trump blond, busty, hemp-wearing Johanna for my mom's affections, Dad still loved mom desperately, and I think he believed in his heart of hearts that they could make it work. I wished he could figure out how to move on.

He popped up out of his Downward Dog and said, "How much homework do you have? Want to watch a James Bond marathon? We can order Chinese. Have a little post-birthday celebration. Your sister isn't due home for hours, so let's have some fun. Just the two of us."

"Sounds great," I said. But as I watched my dad roll up his

yoga mat and stuff it under the couch, I thought about what we used to do for fun as a family: play soccer in the park, go for walks along the creek near our house, get together with other families for dinner or games. Why didn't we do that anymore? Were my dad and I really supposed to just shrivel up into overbaked couch potatoes without my mom there to organize activities for us? "Actually, Dad . . . what do you think about going out?"

"Out?" he asked, scowling. He glanced down at his tank top and flannel pants.

"Yeah, like out to dinner. We could meet up with friends, maybe? Or head to the park and try to get a game of soccer going or something?"

He looked at me like I was an alien. "Why would we do that?"

I shook my head. He was right—why would we do that? I wanted to answer: *So you'll have a social life again* or *So you can show Mom that life goes on without her*. But who was I to talk? I'd stopped doing most of the things I used to do after Velvet ditched me, just like Dad had after Mom left. Without Velvet around to tell me what we had planned, I didn't really do much of anything. Jonathan and Anji were mostly school friends still.

We hadn't hung out on the weekends that much. And I wasn't involved in any after-school activities. Going to the party at Velvet's had been a pretty big deal. "I don't know," I finally said. "It was just an idea. But maybe we should watch a movie."

"That's my girl," Dad said with a silly wink. As I got the movie ready, he ran upstairs to change out of his tank top (a relief, trust me). When he came back down, he was holding a folded sheet of paper. "Open it."

I took the paper in my hands and slid my fingernail under the tape that held it closed. Inside was a picture of a lunar eclipse.

"I borrowed a good camera from a guy at work and drove up to the cliffs to take this picture last night," he said, beaming. "I'm going to get it blown-up and framed for your room. Your birthday eclipse."

"I love it," I said, hugging him tight. I glanced over Dad's shoulder at the picture in my hand as I squeezed him. It was perfect. But even still, I found it hard to shake off the creepy feeling that oozed over me whenever I thought about my birthday night. I couldn't tell Dad about the weird missing hour on Velvet's roof or he'd never let me out of the house again. So I just settled into my end of the couch for some James Bond action, wondering if I'd ever know the truth about what had happened to me on the night of my thirteenth birthday.

We were still on the couch several hours later when my mom called. "Happy birthday, baby. I tried you yesterday, but I guess you were off doing something fun?"

I had seen Mom's call come through as I was getting ready for Velvet's party, but I'd ignored it. Even after our summer of bonding in Sweden, I was still upset with her. The way she'd announced the divorce last spring had stung, and I hated that she expected me to understand.

There had been only two weeks left of sixth grade when Mom had called all of us into the living room for a family meeting. Family meetings were common and usually a little random, so I hadn't been expecting much. At one family meeting, Mom had introduced the idea of adding more kale to our diet. During another she'd warned us that Mercury was in retrograde, so we all needed to work harder to be kind to one another.

That night, Mom had held Dad's hand, closed her eyes in a Zen-like way, and said: "Kids, I—*we*—need to talk to you about something." The kale conversation had started the same way so, honestly, divorce was the furthest thing from my mind.

The only thing I could think about was the tacos we were having for dinner. Taco night was the only time my mom let us eat meat, and I was starving.

"Your father and I have decided to go down different paths throughout the rest of our journeys in this life." I glanced at my dad as Mom spewed out her soothing-sounding words. The look on his face told me that whatever this was, it wasn't a *we* decision. It was an *I* decision. "Though I love your father dearly, and he will forever remain a part of me . . ." That's when Mom gazed at Dad and placed a soft kiss on his stubbly cheek. "My heart is pulling me to Sweden."

My eyes bugged out of my head. "Like, IKEA?"

This got a small laugh from my mom. Romy gave me a look that made me zip it. Quick.

"I met a woman named Johanna, and we have discovered we're spiritual soul mates. We complete each other." Tears leaked from my mom's eyes, but a smile was spread wide across her face. Some lady named Johanna had my mom happy-crying.

It was Romy's turn to gape. "Johanna? Spiritual soul mate?" She spat this out with all the sweetness and warmth of a dirt-flavored Popsicle.

"Lucia . . . Romy . . . I'm in love!" Mom gushed. "I know

this is a hard time for me to leave you, considering you're both on the brink of womanhood, but I hope you'll understand that I need to follow the life that's calling to me. In order to give completely, we must first nourish our own selves."

Dad dropped Mom's hand. He wiped his palm on his khakis and cringed as he attempted a weak smile. "What your mom is trying to say is, she's decided to move to Sweden for a while—to live with this *Johanna*—and we're all supposed to be happy for her. She and I are getting a divorce."

That's what she was trying to say? I needed a translator to help me understand my own mom, and she was speaking English. I wondered if she would be easier to understand in Swedish.

"Let me get this straight," Romy growled, her arms crossed. "You're telling us you're gay?"

"There's no need to define it, dear. I'm telling you I'm in love."

"With a woman?"

"Yes. Johanna lives in the northern part of Sweden. Apparently her village is very beautiful."

"And you're moving there?" Romy's lip curled into a sneer. "Leaving us?"

My head whipped back and forth between my mom and my sister. While my dad and I steered away from conflict, they both loved to hash things out in the heat of the moment. I envied them, frankly. At the first sign of a fight, my tongue swelled up and refused to move. But there were plenty of times I would have given anything to be the sort of person who could blurt out exactly what I was thinking. I just didn't have it in me.

Less conflict, more Zen. Or something like that.

Mom took a deep, cleansing breath. "Johanna and I met several years ago at a yoga retreat. We've kept in contact since then and over this past year, our relationship has deepened into something—"

That's when Romy covered her ears and screamed. Really screamed. Sixteen years old with the lungs of a tantrum-prone toddler. Lucky for me, my sister was dramatic enough to get the message across for both of us. She screeched, "Gah! Mom, just stop talking! You have got to be freaking kidding me right now."

Mom, of course, stepped forward and pulled both of us into a hug. I didn't think a hug could cool the sting, but it did. Locked in my mom's embrace, I felt myself stiffen, freeze. My body went numb. Our parents—seemingly without Dad's input or approval—were getting divorced. Mom was in love with a Swedish yogi named Johanna, and she was ditching her family to move to the land of blond hair and furniture-store meatballs.

Romy freaked and hollered and slammed her bedroom door. Mom chased after her, begging her to talk through it, reminding her that bottling up her emotions was toxic. Meanwhile, I silently stewed and watched old TV shows with Dad, neither of us saying anything to the other. There was really nothing to say. Instead of tacos we ate microwave dinners and left the veggies uneaten, glistening with congealed butter in their little cardboard compartment. This was our way of lashing out.

Life moved fast after the big announcement. Mom packed up in a hurry, explaining—over and over again—that her move wasn't permanent. She would come back home after a year (presumably with Johanna, if things worked out) but needed to take a little time for herself. To align her chi. Never mind the fact that she was leaving my chi in pieces.

Through the remaining days of sixth grade, I did my best to smile and be supportive. I hoped that if I stayed positive, it might ease the transition (for her *and* for me). There's always a rainbow at the end of a bad storm.

Every cloud has a silver lining.

The best is yet to come.

Here's the honest truth: I've never been a big believer in any of the positive-energy stuff my mom always yammers on about. But I put up a good front. Everyone likes a nice girl with a good attitude. No one ever wants to hear the truth.

Then came the kicker. Instead of celebrating the last day of school with our usual ice cream and a family hike by the river, my mom surprised us with the news that Romy and I would be joining her for the next two months in a small village outside the town of Kiruna, Sweden. She felt it was important that we get to know Johanna and adjust to this new life. No one seemed to realize that spending the summer with my mom and her new girlfriend in a strange land was not going to help me adjust to anything, except bitterness. Romy protested so much—and pulled the summer-job card—that she got out of it.

Me? I went. I just couldn't put up a fight. How was I supposed to know that everything would break into even more pieces while I was gone?

Over the summer I discovered that Johanna was nice and everything. But two months with my new "family" wasn't enough to convince me to accept Mom's change of heart with open arms and confetti. I wanted her to explain herself, to tell me what was so wrong with the life she had that she had to move across the ocean to build a new one.

Now that I was home again, and Mom was still an ocean away, I could always feel the miles that stretched out between us when she called. There was a short silence; then Mom said, "Yesterday was a big birthday, sweetie. Do you feel like you've come of age?" *Gag.* Mom had been all hopped up on buzz-words like this since her latest yoga retreat, and they weren't helping me forgive her any faster.

"Sure, Mom. It's like I'm finally whole." I looked down, fully aware that nothing had changed. Nonexistent bust, the same pj pants I'd had since I was ten and hit a growth spurt, and my dad's old KISS T-shirt. I was a real woman now.

She paused. "Really, sweetheart?" I swear I could hear the tears flowing. "I wish I could have been there with you for this." I could almost smell her "relax" tea blend through the phone. Mom was overly sentimental and emotional about everything now that she wasn't here for our day-to-day lives. I often wished I could tell her that that's what you get when you walk out on a family.

"No, not really, Mom. No worries, you're not missing

much—except I can read minds now. But I told you that, right?"

"That's not funny, Lucia. Did you get the book I sent? It made it in time?"

Mom gave me a book of some sort of bunk magic every year, and this year was no exception. My thirteenth birthday book was *Legends of Shadow and Light*. "Yeah, Mom, I got it. Looks like a good one." I wondered if she could sense the sarcasm in my voice. Doubtful. In fact, I could hear her sniffling happily on the other end of the line.

But I definitely did *not* love the book she had sent. Just like every year, I had stuffed the book deep under my bed and hoped none of its creepy magic content would seep up from under my metal bed frame. I didn't think that was really possible, but I wasn't willing to risk it. Mom's paranormal nonsense freaked me out. The woman had given me a *moonstone* because I was born during an eclipse, for goodness' sake—you can't get more superstitious than that. It's not like the moon was going to steal me up into the sky and take me off to Lunar Landing.

As I waited for Mom to stop weeping on the other end of the phone, I wandered over to the front hall and pulled the moonstone out of my jacket pocket. My dad rolled his eyes when he saw me cupping it in my palm—he was on my team when it came to Mom's magic worship. I rolled my eyes back at him, and then looked down at the rock in my palm. My eyes widened, and my heart began to beat faster. Something about the stone had changed.

The moonstone had always been just a solid, pearly white—but now there was a black vein running through it that made it look like the rock had split open. My palms were sweating, and a cold chill passed over me as I stared at the changed stone. The shadowy black core hadn't been there when I'd pulled it out at the grocery store before Velvet's party. When had it changed?

"Do you feel any different?" Mom prodded. "Did you get a chance to see the eclipse last night? I've been waiting to call since I figured you'd be sleeping in this morning."

"No, yes, and thanks." My heart was beating furiously. I stared at the moonstone, realizing I suddenly did *not* feel well.

Mom laughed. "Very detailed. Seriously, Lucia . . . Is everything okay?" I could hear a catch in her voice, as if there was something specific she wanted to ask me. "Did you—"

"Everything's fine, Mom," I snapped, cutting her off. I didn't want to have to lie to her about what had happened, which meant I couldn't let her press. "The eclipse was cool." The lie rolled off my tongue, and I waited for the moonstone to burn my hand or something. You'd figure that's what would happen. It didn't.

"Okay." She sounded disappointed. Was she was expecting some other answer? It was tough to analyze someone's words when you couldn't see their facial expressions. Also, I had had a hard time believing much of what my mom said after we found out most of her life had been a lie.

"How's Johanna?" I asked, steering the conversation in a new direction. I wrapped my fingers around the stone, hoping that if I couldn't see it, I would forget about it. Pieces of last night's bizarre dream kept flitting through my brain, a constant reminder that something strange had happened during the eclipse.

Mom sighed, as though she had more to say but didn't want to push it. "She's wonderful. We're thinking of going back up to the north of Norway next month for another visit. Our last retreat was so relaxing, and I love the legends of the tribes up there. They're so captivating, and few are in written record—so we're digging into the verbal history slowly . . ." I zoned out. A few minutes later we said good-bye, and she promised to call in a day or two.

After we hung up, I shoved the rock—that's all it was, a

rock—into my hoodie pocket and vowed not to think about it anymore. I didn't believe in Mom's magic crap, and I certainly wasn't going to believe that stupid rock had changed overnight. It was ridiculous. Obviously, I had just never noticed the dark vein before. Maybe it was a trick of the light. That was the only logical explanation. Even so, my stomach was knotted and uneasy for the rest of the afternoon.

CHAPTER SIX

An embarrassing number of hours into our TV marathon I went upstairs to change out of my pajama pants. It seemed a little pointless to change out of jammies when I was going to have to get back into them a few hours later, but getting dressed for even a little while gave my day the structure I so badly needed. It was one little thing that made me feel more in control of my life after everything that had happened over the last few months.

In the bathroom I left the light off so I could look out the window at Will's house while I brushed my teeth. Like some sort of creepy Peeping Tom, I peered out into the twilight. I tucked deeper into the shadows when I noticed Will was out there, dragging a bag of garbage toward the can in the Bartons' backyard.

He obviously hadn't left yet to meet Velvet and everyone else for the get-together at Jake's. The river behind Jake's house was only a few blocks from my house. I loved walking along the river path during the day, especially in the fall when the ground was covered with leaves and clusters of pine needles. Will and I had spent hours at the river as kids, exploring for bugs under rocks and trying to catch fish with our bare hands. When we were eight or nine, we spent most of the summer trying to work up the nerve to jump off the bridge that crossed over the swimming hole. Finally, after a hundred times chickening out, I did it—and survived. It took Will another three weeks before he worked up the nerve. By the end of summer we would jump over and over again, and then dry off slowly as we wandered through the woods back toward home.

Tonight the river would have a different vibe. I could picture them, Velvet's friends and Will's friends, settled in on the rocky embankment with a campfire hidden from the path that ran overhead.

Through the open window I heard Will's cell phone ring and wondered if it was Velvet, checking up on him to see when he'd be leaving. The conversation was short and his voice too low to carry the words all the way to me. I heard him laugh about something, and I was suddenly overcome with jealousy and sadness. I missed making him laugh like that. I wanted my friend back.

Will heaved the bag into the plastic can and turned back toward his house. But then he changed course and made his way toward the tree house. He put his foot on the second rung and pulled himself up. For years Will's tree house had been the place we went to escape. It was a fortress when—as four-year-olds—Will and I had convinced ourselves there were neighborhood trolls hunting for children to eat. At seven, he and I hid from Owen Marshall and the neighborhood fourth graders. For the past few years we had spent most of our time up there listening to music and talking.

It was my safe place, miles away from the real world and family and school drama. Without Will and our hiding place, I would never have survived the weeks leading up to the divorce last spring. It's where I had gone to cry after my mom had surprised me with the news about my summer trip to Sweden.

"When do you leave?" Will had asked that night after the last day of school, tossing a plastic baggie of cookies into my lap. Unlike my house, Will's was always filled with homemade goodies.

"Three days."

"It's a little exciting, though. Sweden."

I shrugged. "I guess. A once in a lifetime experience, as my mom keeps saying. An escape from New York and a chance to see the world. I'm sure she thinks that's a selling point." I crumpled up one of Will's old fleece jackets to use as a pillow. I closed my eyes, listening to the sounds of chickadees warbling in the trees around us. A lone cardinal called for its mate. Will and I had studied birdcalls the summer between second and third grade, one of our many summer projects. A project Velvet had teased me incessantly about when I'd told her about it. "I never thought my first trip to Europe would be with my mom and her new girlfriend."

Will snorted. "Yeah." He nudged my shoulder with his knee. "It's gonna be okay."

I nodded. "Yeah."

"Lucia . . ." I could hear him breathing beside me. After a long silence, I opened my eyes. He was looking at me with a half smile on his face. Tears bloomed in my eyes and I slammed them closed again. He said feebly, "It's just a couple of months. It's not like you're leaving forever."

Sitting there that day, I'd wondered how I could explain that it wasn't the next two months in Sweden that worried me. I wasn't like Velvet or Romy, worrying that I'd miss something important during the time that I was away. It wasn't that. It was the permanence of the rest of it. Not those two months, but the rest of my life. Everything was changing, and I hated it. I was angry with my mom and frustrated with my dad for not fighting harder. I resented my sister because she always had the guts to say what she was thinking. And I hated myself for pretending everything would be okay.

After a long silence Will had finally said, "I get it, though. I'm mad too." Simple as that, I knew he understood. I sat up and we leaned against each other. Back to back, I felt safe.

Now, a few months and a whole lot of changes later, I stared out the window at his tree house again. I yawned, and a glop of toothpaste dropped from my mouth to my T-shirt. I bent over to wipe it off with my thumb, and when I looked out the window again, Will was staring straight up at me. He lifted a hand to wave. Like a fool, I dropped to the ground and crawled out of the bathroom on all fours, my mouth still full of paste.

Romy, who had finally come home from her friend's house, stared at me as I scuttled past her in the hall. "Lu, you're only making life harder for yourself by acting like a freak," she said, peering down at me.

I crawled into my bedroom, then spit the toothpaste into a tissue and dumped it in the trash. I swished with some water from the glass I kept next to my bed. When I looked up again, my sister was staring at me like I'd grown a third arm or suddenly begun to float. "What?"

She shook her head. "Did you just spit your toothpaste into the trash?"

"Maybe."

Romy tossed her chestnut-colored hair over her shoulder and asked, "*How* is it possible we're related?"

"Well, the way it works is this . . ." I settled in on the floor of my room and smiled up at her. I spoke in a slow, dopey voice I knew my sister hated. "Mom and Dad had you first. You were such a delightful baby that they decided they should have another little bundle of joy who could keep you company. So a few years later, they had me. When I was born—thirteen years and one day ago, exactly—I became your sister!" I blinked at her. "In case you'd forgotten, it was my birthday yesterday. The anniversary of the day *you* became a big sister."

"Whatever. Congratulations to me on the big anniversary."

Romy rolled her eyes. "Can you keep Dad occupied tonight? I'm meeting up with some friends, and if he's engrossed in TV, he won't even notice me leaving."

"Not even a happy birthday?" I prompted, tilting my head. "You're just going to ask for the favor, without buttering me up at *all*?"

Romy twirled a strand of her hair around her finger and glared at me. Once upon a time, the two of us were actually quite close. Though my sister and I were always polar opposites, we were far enough apart in age that it never really mattered. She had loved dressing me up in silly little outfits when I was in preschool, and she would give me a discounted rate of twenty-five cents per hairstyle at the neighborhood salon she started with a friend. We used to love playing in hotel pools together on family road trips, and she would read me chapter books aloud during her elementary school read-a-thon.

But after my mom's announcement last spring, my sister had become so self-absorbed that she actually sucked the life out of everyone around her. Though she would never admit it, I'm pretty sure Romy had taken the divorce harder than anyone. I don't know why she was taking her anger out on me, but it wasn't fair. I always sort of wished she and I could be the kind of sisters who would sit up late, chatting about how our lives had changed, and help each other deal with stuff. We were going through the same thing with the divorce, and I longed to talk to her about it. But instead, she turned into the kind of sister who forgot birthdays and closed her door whenever she was home. For a brief moment I considered telling Romy about what had happened the night before at Velvet's party, but we just didn't have that kind of relationship anymore.

Romy crossed her arms and blurted out, "Don't be lame, Lucia. Just cover for me if Dad asks where I am, okay? Distract him or something."

"What if I'm going out too?" I asked. "Maybe I need *you* to cover for *me*."

Romy laughed. "Unlikely. You and Dad never go anywhere. Just do it, okay?"

"Fine," I grumbled. She flashed me a quick smile, then disappeared. I stood up and looked out at the backyard from my bedroom window. I caught a flash of movement in the tree house and wished—once again—that I had the guts to go out there and talk to Will. If I had nerves like my sister or Velvet or Anji, I would climb up into the tree house and say just the right thing to make our friendship go back to the way it once was. But I wasn't my sister or Velvet or Anji. I was a chicken.

So instead, I went back downstairs and plunked down next to my dad on the couch. I fell asleep in front of the TV not long after and spent the night dreaming of Will and the river and our tree house and a night I wished were real.

OUT OF THE SHADOWS

The moon crawled over the horizon, orange and full like a ripe peach in the ink-black sky. The girl climbed up the ladder to the tree house, where the boy was waiting.

"Hey," he said, grinning. "I'm glad you came. It hasn't been the same up here without you." He pulled a plastic baggie from his sweatshirt pocket and offered her a smushed cookie. "Broken, but just as good," he promised.

She took a bite and swooned, the sharp coolness of mint surprising inside the sugary sweetness of the chocolate cookie. She'd missed these cookies. She'd missed him.

"Are you allowed to be up here with me?" she asked after a moment. Teasing, she said, "Won't your girlfriend be mad? Are you supposed to share these cookies with another girl?"

He laughed. "I don't know. But she doesn't own me—or my mom's baked goods."

For a while they sat together, talking and laughing just like old times. They talked about the bad-idea kiss and everything that had happened that summer, and in no time the strangeness was forgotten. She realized she had been a fool to let someone else scare her away. She had been wrong to let their friendship fall apart so easily.

"I'm meeting up with some people down at the river tonight," he said after a while. "We're all hanging out near Jake's house. Want to come?"

Without a moment's hesitation, she nodded. "For sure."

"Think it's too cold to swim while we're there?" A smile tugged at one corner of his mouth. "Or are you chicken?"

"Me, chicken?" She laughed. "Not a chance."

A short time later the two of them stood together on the rail of the bridge. Her hair whipped around her shoulders like a cape. There were shouts of caution from below, but the wind carried them away. Their warnings didn't scare her. Out of the shadows, she felt invincible.

"On three?" she asked.

"One," he said.

"Two," she answered.

"Three." Together, they jumped.

CHAPTER SEVEN

When I woke the next morning, I was tangled up in my covers and still fully dressed. I found my sneakers, damp and muddy, on the floor beside my bed . . . but had no idea how they'd gotten there, or why they were wet.

My head felt like it was stuffed with shadows, so I set off to the river for a walk. I hadn't slept well, and the combination of my changed moonstone and the wet sneakers beside my bed had me really freaked out. I hoped a walk might clear my mind.

Overnight the temperature had dropped. My leather jacket was missing from its usual hook by the door. I had a feeling Romy had taken it again. Even though Mom had told me I could have it when I found it in one of her boxes of stuff last spring, my sister and I had been fighting over it since I got back from Sweden. I couldn't handle a confrontation with Romy that morning, so I went without. I stepped outside and shivered in the cooler autumn air.

I hustled down the deserted sidewalk toward the path along the river. While I walked, I reached my hand into my sweatshirt pocket and rubbed my thumb across the moonstone again. Flashes of last night's dream popped into my head, jumbled images of the river and Will and the footbridge I was crossing now. The scene felt so real. I wished for a moment that it were more than just a dream.

My foot slipped as I climbed down the steep incline that led to the water, and I realized for the first time just how deserted this little piece of the world was. If I fell, there would be no one to hear me scream. The houses on the other side of the river were set far back from the water, and the dense trees made it feel like I was in the middle of a deep, dark forest. One misstep and I could slip into the water and be whisked off into nothingness. I was totally alone.

In the slanted morning sun, shadows cast by falling leaves made me think of ghosts passing through, leaving little puffs of wind in their wake. The sound they made as they dropped to the ground was like tiny footsteps, and suddenly I was haunted by the thought that someone could be following me. The someone who had left wet sneakers beside my bed. Every sound made me jump, and a squirrel that dashed across my path elicited a tiny scream that left me shaken.

When real footsteps thudded behind me, I froze. A girl in Romy's class jogged past a moment later. She waved, and I laughed and tried to act like I hadn't been scared half out of my skin just moments before. I turned around and headed back toward home—this was ridiculous. I was getting frightened over nothing.

As I approached the bridge and prepared to climb back up to the road, I noticed something dark on the bank alongside the river. It looked a lot like my leather jacket, so I climbed under the bridge to investigate.

"She is evil," I muttered, automatically blaming my sister as I reached for the jacket stuffed behind one of the rocks that sat along the water's edge. There were scattered remnants of a campfire from the night before, and soda bottles and candy wrappers littered the ground. Were Romy and her friends at the river sometime last night too? Obviously they had been, and my sister had ditched my leather jacket while she was there.

I put it on and shoved my hands in the pockets to warm up as I climbed the hill toward home. I grinned as I felt a cell phone in the pocket and celebrated the fact that I had proof my sister had stolen my jacket. I could hold her phone ransom until she apologized. Romy wasn't the kind of girl who could even pronounce the word "sorry" anymore, so this would be fun. I pulled her phone out to read through what were sure to be millions of missed text messages, and then I realized it was *my* phone in the pocket. I felt my hands go numb, and a cold flash rushed over me. Had *Romy* taken my jacket and cell phone, or . . .

I shook off the thought with an angry toss of my head and tucked my chin against my chest to rush home.

As soon as I got inside, I stormed upstairs and dug under my bed. I looked at the years of my life, stacked up in a pile of books. For my fifth birthday, the first year mom had given me one of her supernatural books, I'd received *Mystic Mayhem*. I had spent a few minutes with her reading that one aloud to me, before I stuffed the book under my bed because it creeped me out. I pulled *Mystic Mayhem* out now and paged through it. I also pulled out *Vampire & Werewolf Lore* and set it on my bed alongside *Astrological Splendor* and all the other weirdo titles that had collected in my room over the years.

The books were mostly text, with a few crazy photos that were obviously photoshopped to prove some point in the book—a picture of Bigfoot (just a guy dressed up in a really crappy Halloween Superstore bear costume), an image of a glowing orb spotted near the Arctic Circle (even *I* can make spots appear on my pictures and I don't own a fancy camera—it's called bad photography), a photo of some woman concentrating really hard on something while her hands floated "mysteriously" above a table.

I paged through each of the books, skimming past chapters on ghost hunters, psychics, and angels. Frustrated, I flopped back onto my bed and pushed the books onto the floor. The whole pile of them thudded against the carpet with a satisfying thunk. I closed my eyes, forcing myself to calm down. After all, there was a rational explanation for everything, right?

Wrong.

First, there was the matter of the missing hour at Velvet's.

Then there was my moonstone—why and when had it changed? It was as if my mom was playing a joke on me somehow.

Now I had a pair of wet shoes and a jacket and cell phone that had somehow ended up at the river . . . and the dream that seemed somehow connected.

None of this made any sense.

I hated that my apparent insanity was driving me to search through the unreliable nonsense that my mom and her friends were into. As if some stupid, made-up book was going to tell me what was going on.

The pile of books lay helter-skelter on the rug, and when I looked down at them again, I saw that one of the books had flipped open when it crashed to the floor. I inched my torso off the bed and leaned in closer to see what was on the page. As I did, my moonstone slipped out of my pocket and landed on the book. My body tensed, and I felt my arm hair stand on end. Caught up in the magic of the moment, I wondered what that weird rock had to do with everything. It seemed like it was talking to me by landing on the page.

This one open page is going to give me all the answers, I thought. The moonstone falling into the book's open arms, the conveniently open page—it had to be a sign. I was about to get a sign!

My eyes scanned the page, alert and ready. "'Table of

Contents'?" I muttered aloud. "Well, that's a crappy sign." I had never liked surprises, and my life was turning into a fat cluster of them without my prior approval or planning. Some people might be okay with that, but as for me? I do *not* like to not be in control.

CHAPTER EIGHT

knew it was going to be a wonderful week when, on Monday morning, the man sitting across from me on the bus was holding a big silver toenail clipper and looked ready to use it. His shoes were off, placed neatly on the seat next to him. The guy squeezed, and a clipped toenail crescent flew up into the air. It twisted and flipped before landing right in my favorite travel mug with a delicate plunk. I shrieked and shot him an evil look, but he was too busy inspecting his foot to notice.

When I got off the bus, I tossed my cocoa and the cup in the trash can on the corner across from school. It wasn't the first time something like this had happened. I'd been on the bus with that guy three times since school started, and each time he'd been doing something off. Clipping his nails, trimming his mustache with a pair of mini scissors. The first day of school he spent the whole ride working on a zit before the stuff inside squirted out and shot across the aisle. I had tried sitting in different parts of the bus, but the guy always seemed to find an open seat near me where I'd have a perfect view of his disgusting public transportation habits.

These were the hazards of taking the city bus to school. Our school district rezoned at the end of last year, and my elementary school was divided up between Hudson and another middle school on the far end of town. My block was officially reassigned to the other middle school, which meant there was no longer a Hudson school bus stop near my house. Will had convinced his parents to let him go to Hudson because it's where his whole soccer team had ended up. I had begged my parents to let me open enroll there because it's where Velvet and Will were going. I'd researched city bus routes in the spring when school choice cards were due and explained that I didn't want to start middle school friendless and alone. By the time I realized Velvet (along with the other Chosen Ones) had ditched me and Will and I were no longer really speaking, it was too late to switch schools for a fresh start.

I walked the two blocks from the bus stop to school slowly, my feet dragging. I was exhausted. I hadn't slept well since the night of my birthday, and my head was fuzzy and thick with strange thoughts about the weekend and my weird dreams. About a block from school, a car pulled up beside me, and someone yelled, "Hey, Lucia!" It was Will, sticking his head out the backseat window of his mom's car. His mom waved at me; then Will said, "Do you want a ride?"

"We're a block from school," I noted.

"Not today," Will responded, laughing. "I mean, other days. Tomorrow, if you want. Whenever."

His mom yelled, "We're coming from the same place. It's silly for us not to drive you."

I just stared back, my head and mouth unable to nod or form any words. I hadn't even considered asking Will for a ride. Last year it would have made perfect sense to ride together since we still hung out and stuff. But this year it felt weird. And Velvet would be furious. Before I could pull myself together to say no, or smile, or in some way act like a human being, a car honked behind them, and Will's mom sped up to turn into the drop-off circle. Will poked his head out the window and yelled, "That was fun on Saturday night! I'm glad you came."

Certain he must be talking to someone else, I shuffled into school alone.

* * *

"Do you think I should get a ride from him?" I asked Anji and Jonathan at lunch later that day. I picked at my sandwich, not at all interested in eating. With Mom gone, I had created a lunch schedule for myself—Monday: tuna, Tuesday: PB&J, Wednesday: hummus, Thursday: turkey, Friday: bagel. But less than two months into school, I was bored of the routine. I dropped the soggy top slice of bread back on the heap of tuna and sighed. "Or is it too weird? It would be awkward, right?"

Jonathan inserted an entire cookie into his mouth before saying, "If Will Barton is offering you a ride to school, I say you take it. Unless you enjoy the city bus?"

"No, I don't love the bus," I muttered. I quickly told them about toenail guy.

Anji sighed. "Oh, Lucia, why does this kind of thing always happen to you?"

"It's not like I *invite* bad stuff to happen to me! It just happens. I can't do anything about it." I brushed at Jonathan's black T-shirt to clear away the cookie-crumb buffet. I sometimes wondered how much of his food actually made it into his mouth. I mumbled, "I'm sure Velvet would just love it if Will started giving me a ride to school."

"Why do you care so much about what she thinks?" Anji snapped. She dropped her fork into her plastic container and glared at me. "He was your friend first, right? She doesn't own him."

I was so tempted to grab a cookie off Jonathan's stack and shove it into my mouth before he noticed, but I resisted. Instead, I peeled a slice off my clementine and said, "But now he's Velvet's boyfriend. That makes him off-limits."

"I disagree," Jonathan said.

"If you would tell us more about what happened between the two of you, we could help you figure out what would and wouldn't be awkward," Anji said, giving me a look. She sounded annoyed. "That's what friends are for. You tell us things—we help you."

"There's nothing to tell," I lied. "I'm going to tell him thanks but no thanks for the ride. The bus isn't that bad. Now, can we talk about something else?" I begged. "Please?"

"For the record, I think you're being crazy. I just wish you would trust us," Anji said. She shook her head and sighed. "But fine. Subject is changed. Did you guys see the sign-up sheet is posted for the fall musical? They're doing *The Wizard of Oz* this year. Auditions are next week. I'm going to try out."

"You should!" I urged, popping another slice of clementine into my mouth. "I didn't know you were into drama."

"I can't actually sing," Anji said with a laugh. "Which makes a musical kind of a long shot. But I thought it might be fun to try, at least." She cocked her head to one side. "If I made it, though, I don't think my parents would let me do it."

Jonathan groaned. I looked from him to Anji and asked, "Why not?"

"Her parents never let her do anything," he explained.

"That's not true!" Anji argued. "They let me go to Velvet's party last weekend because it was Lucia's birthday. And that was on a Friday!"

"What's wrong with Fridays?" I asked.

"It's 'family night,'" Jonathan said, flicking quote-fingers in the air. "You weren't allowed to go to a movie with me last year on my birthday because it conflicted with family night."

"You have a family night?" I said, surprised I hadn't known this before now. I guess there wasn't a lot of reason for me to know about Anji's family night. But I felt bad that there was this huge thing that I was just learning about now. "I love that!"

Jonathan nodded. "She always whines about it, but she has no idea how lucky she is. Children of divorce don't get a family night." Jonathan's parents were also divorced. He and I hadn't talked about the specifics much, but I had gotten the impression his family situation wasn't pretty.

"I do know how lucky I am," Anji said, digging her fork into her container of leftovers. "And we've talked about your birthday a thousand times. I wasn't allowed to go to a movie with you for your birthday because you're a guy. My parents thought it was inappropriate."

"We've been friends forever," Jonathan said. My head swiveled back and forth between them, fascinated at their bluntness. "Do you think they'll *ever* be okay with us hanging out?"

"They don't *dislike* you," Anji said. "And they don't tell me I can't be friends with you. You just don't get invited over for family night or anything. It would be weird."

Jonathan laughed. "Wow, that's a ringing endorsement." He batted his puppy-dog eyes at her. "I just want to come over for one Mehta dinner. Just one! Your mom's meals sound amazing, and someday I need to see what a happy family night is like. Is that too much to ask?"

"I'll keep working on it, you big whiner." Anji punched him in the arm. "Can we get back to the auditions?"

Jonathan flashed me a smile, then nodded at her. "Of course, Your Highness."

Through a mouthful of food, Anji said, "I really am a terrible singer. But I figure, what's the worst that could happen?"

Total humiliation, I thought, but didn't say that aloud. "I loved doing plays when I was a kid," I admitted. "My sister was in the Hudson musical when she was in eighth grade and said it was super fun. And Romy can be pretty hard to please." The truth was I wished I had the guts to try out for the play. Velvet and I used to write and direct our own plays during the summer when we were little, and I'd always loved getting into character, pretending to be someone else for a while.

"You should try out too," Anji said, clapping. "We can cheer for each other at auditions. And if we both make it, just think of how much fun we would have. Maybe we could be Munchkins together."

"Nuh-uh." I shook my head. "Drama club is Velvet's thing."

"Velvet's thing?" Jonathan groaned. "So you're saying she owns Will *and* drama club?"

I realized this sounded ridiculous. But it was true. Velvet had laid claim to drama club at the end of elementary school, when she was the star in both the fall and spring sixth-grade performances. Once, I'd brought up the idea of trying out. I thought it would be fun to do it with her, even though standing up onstage in front of a crowd was terrifying for me. I figured I'd be okay if I had a friend up there with me for support. But Velvet had convinced me I would be better at behind-the-scenes stuff, like set design (not at all true). So instead of trying out, I spent hours last year helping her learn her lines, never considering that they could have been *my* lines I was memorizing instead of hers. "I'm not really the type," I said lightly, trying to make it sound like it wasn't a big deal. "I'm more of a behind-the-scenes kind of girl."

Anji frowned. She opened her mouth to say something, but before we could talk about it any further, Daunte Adams breezed past our table and smacked me on the shoulder. "*Luuuu*-cia! What's up? That was crazy fun on Saturday, yeah?"

I spun around, wondering when and how Daunte Adams had learned my name. We had a few classes together, sure, but he'd never said one word to me before. My friends and I watched as Daunte weaved his way through the cafeteria and slid into an open seat at Will's table.

"What was *that* about?" Anji asked, gaping at me.

"I don't know," I answered honestly. I snuck another quick

glance at Will's table, then let my gaze slide to the table filled with the Chosen Ones next to them. Velvet and her friends were all glaring at me. One of them laughed at something Velvet said, and then, out of the corner of my eye, I saw Velvet stand up and come my way.

"Velvet's coming over here," Anji said under her breath. "Why?"

I shrugged, and a moment later Velvet plopped down on the bench next to me. She turned up her nose at my tuna and pushed it across the table. Her friends Briana Rosen and Mariah Vandenburg sauntered up and stood at attention on either side of her. They were the scrawniest bodyguards I'd ever seen.

Velvet smoothed her short black skirt over the striped tights I'd always envied. "So," she said sweetly. "I had a thought." The way she said this made it sound like we were in the middle of a conversation. "I'm going to introduce you to Jeremy Hiller. I think you guys would be cute together."

"Wha—?" Jonathan said, spluttering. "You want to set Lucia up?" Anji laughed, and I considered joining her.

Velvet turned her attention to Jonathan for a fraction of a second. "This is your business *how*?"

Eager to avoid a fight, I spoke up. "Jeremy Hiller is my Spanish partner. I know him already."

Velvet laughed. "Perfect. Then it will be ideal."

I wanted to tell her that Jeremy Hiller smelled like dirty feet and vegetable soup and that I would never, ever be interested in him. But before I could say anything, Anji blurted out, "So I had a thought too. It's this: *I* think you should butt out of Lucia's business."

"Oh you do, do you?" Velvet said, arching an eyebrow. She looked over at me and smiled coolly. "I see you've found someone else to speak up on your behalf, Lucia. Well done." She continued to look at me, even when she said to Anji, "Well, whatever-your-name-is, perhaps you could remind Lucia that she should probably *butt out* of my business too, then. Stay away from Will. I don't know what you think you're doing, but your little stunt at the river was pitiful. Just give up. Got it?"

As she walked away, I could actually feel the blood drain from my face, and a cold, clammy feeling seeped over my skin. Panicking, I thought back to the dream I'd had that weekend: Will, the tree house, the river. Then I thought about my jacket, and the wet shoes, and what Will had said to me before school that morning. I thought about the black streak in my moonstone, and my birthday eclipse, and the way Velvet had acted when I woke up on the strange part of her roof that night—like I had missed something.

"What little stunt at the river?" Jonathan whispered in a rush.

"When were you at the river with Velvet?" Anji demanded.

The lunch bell rang, and I slowly stood up without answering them. I felt light-headed and grabbed on to the edge of the table for support.

"Lucia?" Jonathan asked, taking my arm. "Are you okay?"

"Talk to us," Anji demanded.

I knew I had to tell someone what was happening. But what *was* happening? None of this made any sense. "I'm fine," I said lightly. "Just tired." I was tired, but I was obviously not fine. In fact, I was pretty sure I was going crazy. Ever since the night of my thirteenth birthday, it felt like I had some serious catching up to do . . . with myself.

CHAPTER NINE

A s soon as I got home from school that afternoon, I went online to search for information about sleep-walking, hallucinations, weird dreams . . . anything that could rationally explain what was happening with me. There was a lot of information out there, and none of it seemed to fit what was going on. Sleepwalking seemed unlikely, as did hallucinations.

Then I stumbled upon an article that talked about something called multiple personality disorder. I was sucked in. Some of the symptoms were terrifyingly familiar to what I'd been experiencing: sleep problems, flashbacks, missing time. There were a bunch of things that didn't ring true for me—depression, anxiety, and other really serious stuff—but within minutes I'd read enough to start getting myself even more scared.

And the more I learned, the more I was convinced I shouldn't tell anyone anything about my lost hours. I didn't think I was actually going crazy, but the possibility terrified me. Scared me senseless, I guess. What if they locked me up in an institution?

As I frantically paged through more and more search results, my mom called in on Skype. I felt super guilty I hadn't yet told her anything about the eclipse or the changed moonstone or the absurdly real dreams and forgotten moments I'd been having since Velvet's party. I didn't really think she would have any sensible explanations, but I longed to talk to her about it—the way I used to talk to her about everything when I was little. Maybe if I figured out why my dreams felt so tied to real life lately, I could figure out some of the other stuff?

"What do you know about dreams?" I asked casually, staring down at my hands to pick at a fingernail. I didn't want to tell Mom much—she was a worrywart by nature and had a tendency to jump to strange conclusions—but I hoped she might have some information that could lead me away from multiple personality disorder.

"I know plenty about dreams," Mom said, staring at me through her webcam. She picked up a mug from some unseen surface and took a sip of what I knew was tea. It almost felt like we were sitting at the kitchen table together, except I couldn't see her pants. Also, there were a few thousand miles and an ocean between us. And obviously the intangible distance that has a tendency to creep in when your mom bails on your life. "Johanna spent several weeks at a dream center in Copenhagen last spring. The dream weavers—that's what they called the course participants—recorded nighttime adventures and spent their days exploring their meaning. Do you need some counseling?"

"I'm just trying to figure out, generally, how much dreams tie back to real life?" I was staring down, suddenly obsessed with my old Mickey Mouse T-shirt. My other hand twisted my tangled mess of hair.

"Have you been having nightmares again?" I peeked up and saw that my mom was staring back at me from the screen with a disturbing level of intensity. She used to look at me like that when I was seven and started having late-to-school dreams every night. I was always an anxious kid. This wasn't exactly the same, but her concern made me feel better somehow. I wondered if I'd tell her more if she still lived nearby.

I chewed a piece of my hair, then spit it back out again.

"No, not bad dreams, necessarily. Lately, it just seems like my dreams have been connecting really closely to stuff happening in real life."

"Is it just dreams, Lucia?" My mom was the one looking down now. We both had a tendency to avert our eyes to keep people from seeing the worry that pulled at our faces. "Has anything strange been going on?"

I felt my heart jump into high gear. It was pounding a mile a minute, running wild. *Yes!* I wanted to scream. *Yes, a lot of strange stuff has been going on.* "I guess . . . ," I said reluctantly. "I don't know. It's no big deal, Mom."

"Lucia, if there's something you're not telling me, I can't figure out the right way to help you." She looked angry. "Have you been keeping your moonstone close, for protection?"

As a matter of fact, I *had* been keeping my moonstone close. For some reason, I wanted it near me more than ever now. Even though I still didn't believe that it actually held any kind of protective power, I wasn't willing to risk it. Especially with everything that had been going on.

"Lucia?" My mom prompted, trying to drag me back to the conversation. "Tell me what else is worrying you."

She couldn't force me to tell her anything more. She'd lost

that right when she flew the coop. I had to do some more research on my own before I was going to confide in her. After all, nothing bad had happened. Velvet was mad at me, no surprise there . . . but it seemed like Will and I were sort of becoming friends again. It was almost as if one of my birthday-eclipse wishes was trying to come true. But that was silly. You didn't get your wish just *because*—wishes came true with a lot of careful planning and luck, not magic.

Maybe nothing else would happen, and I was worrying for no reason. I was tempted to slam my laptop closed, to show Mom that we were done talking. But I thought better of it, since I knew that closing her out like that would seriously hurt her feelings. Even after what she'd done to us, I didn't have the heart to hurt her back. "I'll call you in a couple days, okay? I think I've just been having too much cocoa before bed or something."

"Okay, baby." She looked unconvinced. "You know, if you don't want to talk to me about it, you could go see my friend Suze. You remember Suze, right?"

Yeah, I remembered Suze. Her house had always smelled like magical nonsense when I was a kid—incense and rose water and something else that made me sneeze. I think I remember that she even had a crystal ball on her coffee table. As *if* I had any intention of talking to Suze.

Mom continued, "She lives near the train station now. I think she lives above that pizza place. Beek's?" She laughed, and I joined in. "Yeah, there's something amusing about someone like Suze living above a pizza place. It all sounds so quaint and inspiring, doesn't it? But her boyfriend is a grad student, so neither of them is really rolling in dough." She wiggled her eyebrows at me. "Get it? Dough? Pizza dough?"

I shook my head. "Yeah, Mom. Good one. Her boyfriend is a grad student?" I said, still amused by the image of hennaed, scarf-wrapped Suze grabbing a slice of pepperoni for lunch every day. "How old is he?"

"Old for Suze." Mom laughed. "I think this one's twenty-eight."

"Isn't Suze, like, fifty?"

"She's fortysomething. Suze is interesting—but she has some good insights on dreams and memory and shadows."

"Shadows?" I stared at Mickey Mouse on my T-shirt again. "Why shadows?"

Mom shrugged. "She's big on things like light and dark and dream states—you might actually find some of it interesting.

102

Considering your moonstone and the eclipse and all, you might enjoy talking to her. I'll e-mail you her number."

We hung up, but I kept thinking about our conversation. Shadows, dream states, memories. My moonstone. Light, dark, the eclipse . . .

I took a deep breath and dug under my bed, open once again to the idea that maybe one of my mom's books would hold some clues. I finally found a book with a passage on moonstones, so I lay down to read with the little guide propped up on my stomach. Apparently, in India, moonstones were sometimes thought of as dream stones. They were supposed to bring beautiful visions at night. I thought about the dreams I'd had this weekend and had to admit that they were beautiful. Dreams were one thing—but elements of my dreams seemed to be real. *That* was the problem.

"Why are you reading that?" My sister was standing in the door of my room, scanning the collection of magic books strewn around my bed.

I sat up, slightly embarrassed, and said, "Curious, I guess."

Romy came closer and grabbed the book out of my hands. She read aloud, "'A moonstone symbolizes a person's being. It is said to strengthen emotions and give power to a person's subconscious.'" She broke off and looked at me. "Seriously, Lucia?"

My face flushed. "It's interesting," I whispered. I had taken my moonstone out of my pocket so I could study it while I was reading. But now, while my sister paged through the book, I shoved the stone deep inside my pocket again. As soon as I touched its smooth surface, my head was filled with images of the river, the tree house, Velvet's rooftop, and Will.

Romy flipped to another page and read, "'If you possess a moonstone, you will be blessed with a more powerful intuition and a greater ability to understand.'" She looked up. "Lucky you."

I smiled weakly. What she had read was absolutely not true for me. I couldn't understand anything. I was more confused than I'd ever been in my life. I hated that my stone had changed sometime during the night of the eclipse, and I wondered what that meant. Was it normal?

Romy tossed the book down on my bed and said, "Happy reading." As she turned to leave my room, I once again considered talking to my sister about what was happening. But she already thought I was a freak, and this would probably make her think I was crazy, too. She'd try to blame whatever was happening to me on the divorce, and that would make her hate Mom even more than she already did. The last thing I needed was to create extra family drama—my job was keeping the peace.

Maybe I was just going through some sort of hormonal rite of passage that everyone else already knew about. Had my mom failed to warn me about some secret female "thing" that happens on your thirteenth birthday? Or was something in me broken?

OUT OF THE SHADOWS

"Want to do something fun?" the girl asked, pushing open the door to her sister's room. Inside, it smelled like cinnamon and hot cocoa and stirred up memories of winter sledding followed by cold nights snuggled up under a blanket together.

The older girl looked up from her homework and frowned. "Probably not." Then she tilted her head, closed her math book, and asked slowly, "But maybe. What do you have in mind?"

"I want to dye my hair." The girl pulled a box of hair dye out from behind her back and wiggled it in the air. "Purple."

"Mom will kill you," the other girl said, laughing. "You're not serious."

With a shrug, the girl said, "I'm totally serious. She left, so she doesn't get a vote, does she? And I bet Dad won't mind."

"What makes you so sure about that?"

"Have you seen old pictures of him from college? He was a walking ad for Manic Panic hair dye." She shrugged. "We can ask him. I bet he'll help too. He needs a distraction."

The older girl studied her carefully. "You're not acting like you. What's wrong?"

"Nothing's wrong. I've always wanted to dye my hair and there's

no time like the present. But I want your help—it'll be more fun if you do it with me. Are you in or out?"

The older girl hopped off her bed and gave her sister a hug for the first time in months. "I'm totally in."

CHAPTER TEN

ey, Anj," I murmured, hastily fiddling with the combination on my locker.

"Good morning, lovely," Anji called, her head stuffed inside her locker. Then she stepped back and gaped at me. "Whoa! I *love* your hair!"

Though I had gone to bed the night before with boring brown hair, when I woke up, my head was covered in deep purplish-black curls that looked a little like they'd been inked with Crayola markers. I had no memory of doing it, but there was the empty box of dye in the garbage and a colorful head of hair—concrete proof that something seriously strange was happening to me. This had obviously been more than just a dream.

After a few minutes of total shock and horror when I first

saw myself in the bathroom mirror, I realized I loved it. I had always longed for purple hair. I'd gone as far as buying that very box of dye last spring, to use as an act of rebellion after my mom's big announcement—but I'd never even had the guts to do something as risky as temporary hair chalk. Even though I loved how it looked, the boldness of colored hair freaked me out. I washed my hair eight times before school that morning. It refused to fade. Looking at the directions on the side of the box, I found out I was stuck with it through at least forty washes.

Anji reached up to touch my colorful new locks. "It's very . . . daring. And loud. Two words I would never usually use to describe you." Anji tilted her head. "But you know what? It suits you."

I slumped back against the bank of lockers and smiled. "Really?" As weird and *un*like me as it was, I felt happy whenever I thought about my new style.

When I'd bumped into my dad in the kitchen that morning, he barely even reacted to the new color. He just tousled my hair, grinned, and said, "I really am a little jealous." I wasn't sure what he meant and why he was acting so nonchalant about my hair changing colors overnight, but as I ate my breakfast, I began to wonder if maybe he'd been with me when I'd dyed it?

I had seen old pictures of my dad from high school and college, and knew he'd been very pro-dye before he met my all-natural mom.

Even stranger, Romy had sauntered into my room on her way to school that morning and dropped one of her favorite green sweaters on my bed. "This will look great with the purple," she promised. Still half-asleep, I squinted up at her and nodded, trying not to grin like a crazy person when she squeezed my shoulder and said, "Have a good day, Lulu. You look gorgeous."

The warning bell rang, and Anji slammed her locker closed. I slipped my hand behind her back and pushed her gently toward the science lab. Science and shop were the only classes Anji was ever on time for, because they were the only classes she and I had together. I was *never* late to class. "I wish I could have been there when you did it," Anji said wistfully. "My parents would *freak* if I colored my hair, so it would have been great to live through you. You're like a whole new Lucia—so fun."

New me. I swallowed back the lump that now seemed to be permanently lodged in my throat. I couldn't help but wonder: Was the old me *not* fun?

* * *

That afternoon in English class we got split up into small groups to discuss *The Strange Case of Dr. Jekyll and Mr. Hyde*, which we were supposed to have finished reading. I guess it was my lucky day—I got paired with Briana, Will, and Velvet. We were told to turn our desks to face one another, like in kindergarten, and discuss the questions on Ms. Tanner-Blank's study sheet.

Velvet stood, waiting for Will to push her desk into place for her.

"I really like your hair," Will said quietly as we rearranged our seats. "Is that the dye you bought last spring? I thought you'd chickened out."

"Yeah, I finally decided to just go for it." I could feel my cheeks flush. I hadn't actually *decided*, though, had I? It seems I'd just gone for it, without ever actually making the decision and without any actual memory of dyeing it. "And thanks, I like it too."

"Do you guys remember when I had a streak of pink in fifth grade?" Velvet asked no one in particular. "I'm so glad I *finally* got rid of all traces of the color. Ugh. It was so ugly and babyish." She sat down at her desk again, waiting for the rest of us to get ourselves in place. "I was so over it."

I'm so over you, I thought, scowling as I sat down across from her. Will snorted, and I suddenly worried I'd accidentally said it aloud.

"So, who's read the book?" Velvet asked.

"I finished it," I said.

"Great, then you can take notes." Velvet smiled. I glared back.

"First question," Briana said, holding the paper close to her face. "What kind of character is Dr. Jekyll when we are first introduced to him? Is he admirable? Is he also flawed?"

"Isn't everyone flawed?" Velvet said, grinning. "Except me, obviously." She laughed, but it sounded forced. When neither Will nor I laughed, Velvet widened her eyes and said, "Come on, you guys, I'm kidding. Lighten up." She brushed her dark hair back from her face and grinned at Will.

"Okay, next question," Briana said. "Do you think everyone has a Mr. Hyde inside themselves?"

Will nodded. "Yeah, isn't the point of the book to say everyone is a little bit good and a little bit evil? Obviously Jekyll and Hyde are kind of extreme examples, but it seems like the author was just saying that everyone has different parts of themselves that come out at different times in their lives." He looked at me. "I mean, there are hidden sides of everyone, right? Things people are hiding from the rest of the world."

"Totally." Velvet nodded. "Are you writing this down, Lucia?"

Will continued, "Everyone has secrets. Secret dreams and wishes that no one knows about. It's just that pieces of our true selves are hidden, waiting for the right time and place to come out." He nodded at me, which made me uncomfortable and nervous until I realized he was holding a plastic baggie with two of his mom's mint chocolate cookies in it. He held the treats under the desks, in the space between our knees, and discreetly dropped one cookie into my hand when I reached out. I set it on my leg to save for later.

Velvet looked over at us and narrowed her eyes.

I broke off a piece of the cookie and popped it into my mouth as Briana read the next question. "Do you believe you really know the people around you—or do you only know part of them?" Briana rolled her eyes. "These are such stupid questions."

"I guess I'd be curious to know what secrets Lucia's been hiding from all of us," Velvet said then. "I've known you your whole life, but I guess I never really realized you had a little rebel tucked inside that shy shell of yours. Showing off at the river last weekend, this weird hair . . . What's next? Are you going to announce you're auditioning for the fall musical, too?" She grinned at me; then she and Briana laughed. Briana kept swiveling her head from side to side, gazing first at Velvet before turning to gauge my reaction.

Velvet knew how uncomfortable this kind of teasing made me. She was trying to make me nervous. What had made me a target for her again? Why was I suddenly worth picking on? I opened my mouth to respond, but Will beat me to it. "Don't be mean, Velvet."

"I'm not being mean!" Velvet said, holding her hands up in surrender. "It's just interesting, don't you think?" She turned to me. "I've known you since you were practically a baby, and I have to say . . . this hair isn't exactly you, is it? You can't really pretend to hide when you're trying so hard to be noticed."

She was right and we both knew it. "Can we just get back to the questions about the book?" I asked.

"I'm sorry if this is making you uncomfortable," Velvet said. "But you can't exactly expect people to ignore you when you so obviously want attention."

"It obviously *is* making her uncomfortable," Will said.

"You don't have to defend me," I blurted out, annoyed that

I always looked (and felt) like a wimp around Velvet. I was sick of letting her pick on me. "I can handle it."

Velvet smiled. "There—see? I know you can, Lucia. And anyway, this is just friendly teasing, Will. Lucia and I are cool. Maybe you could just stay out of it?"

"He's already in it," I whispered under my breath. The bell rang and I took off. The rest of the cookie fell to the floor and was smashed into a brown lump under the weight of my foot.

Quite clearly there was something very strange happening to me, and the easiest way I could think of to deal with it was to simply keep myself distracted . . . and awake.

Though I was exhausted, I knew I couldn't let myself sleep that night. Weird things only seemed to happen when I went to bed, so I decided I had to do everything I could to stay awake for as long as it took for my life to go back to normal. That night, once I was pretty sure my dad and Romy were both asleep, I snuck downstairs and turned on the TV. It was tuned to a channel with a church service where the preacher was extolling the virtues of exorcising your demons. This freaked me out. I'd never been very religious—my dad is Jewish, and my mom Episcopalian. Neither was particularly dedicated to their faith, so they'd decided raising my sister and me as nothing at all would be easier than picking one or worrying about splitting our time between both. We'd gone to church on major holidays and always had a Passover seder with one of Dad's college friends, but that was about it. Now I worried about how little I knew and fretted that I had missed an important lesson that would explain everything in a tidy little passage.

When I couldn't find anything else on TV, I fidgeted with my homework. But writing my essay about *Jekyll and Hyde* felt far too familiar, and I started to panic again. Did I have some sort of split personality, like Dr. Jekyll? Was there something evil lurking within me, my Hyde? Not only was that impossible, it didn't seem likely. I mean, if I were suddenly out killing small dogs and torturing the guy on the bus whose toenail had landed in my cocoa . . . well, that would be a different matter. Could I really consider the unlikely idea that perhaps my personality had split in two? But it's not like you could suddenly go crazy without a catalyst. That kind of stuff sneaks up on you, right?

"Can't sleep?" my dad asked, plunking down on the couch next to me.

"No." I looked up, surprised. I thought he had been asleep for hours. "You either?"

"Nope," he said. "Ever since your mom left, sleep has been a little touch-and-go."

I looked at him. This was the first time he'd really said anything about Mom leaving. Ever since she had informed the family of what was happening, Dad and I had mostly avoided the topic of divorce and moving on. Of course he had asked me about what I'd done in Sweden and tried to get me to spill a few details about Johanna—but he never really complained much or talked about how the divorce had impacted him. He and I were similar in that way. "Popcorn?" he asked.

"Sure." I trailed him to the kitchen and sat at the counter while he got out the air popper and melted some butter. "You haven't been sleeping well?" I asked softly.

"I'll survive," he said, flashing me a smile. He looked away and focused on the popcorn prep. We both sat in silence while the popper whirred and spit out fluffy kernels. When it was done, Dad poured melted butter over the bowl and sprinkled salt over the whole thing. He shoved the bowl across the counter and sighed. "I'd pay good money for one decent night's sleep, though."

"Maybe you need a distraction . . . ," I said through a mouthful of popcorn. "Something to keep your mind off everything?"

"What, like dyeing my hair?" he asked, grinning. He rubbed at the day-old stubble on his chin and shoved his hands into the pockets of his flannel pants. "It looks good, Lucia. Your mom is going to kill me for letting you do it, but the purple looks cool enough that it will be worth the grief."

"Thanks," I said. After a long pause I blurted out, "You're my parent too."

"What?" Dad said, unplugging the popper and putting it back in the cupboard.

"Mom isn't the only one who gets a say," I said, my chest squeezing. "You get to decide some stuff too." I wasn't sure what had made me say this, but as soon as it slipped out, I knew it was the right thing to say.

Dad looked at me and began to nod slowly. "You're right."

A tiny smile tugged at the corners of my mouth. I *was* right.

"You know what, kid? Maybe I should take a cue from you." My dad leaned against the counter. Quietly he added, "Change a few things and take back control of my life." He tossed a handful of popcorn into his mouth and chewed thoughtfully. Then he patted the counter and said, "But right now you and I both need to get up to bed. It's way past lights-out."

"I'm just going to try to finish up this paper for literature class and then I'll go up, okay?" I said.

Dad winked at me, then made his way back up the stairs. "Don't stay up too late, purple girl."

As soon as he was gone and I had the living room to myself again, I thought about what he'd said: that I was changing a few things and taking control of my life. That hadn't been my plan, but when I thought about it, it seemed like that was *exactly* what was happening—whether I liked and planned for it or not. Even though the strange dreams I'd been having were fuzzy and didn't feel like they were based in reality, it was obvious that something about my life was shifting: Will and I were speaking again, my sister had been kind to me on her way to school that morning, I was finally feeling a little less nervous around Velvet, and now I had hair that made me feel like a different person. No matter how scared I felt, I couldn't deny one simple fact: The shattered pieces of my life felt like they had started to shift back into place.

OUT OF THE SHADOWS

"I'm going to do it," the girl said, sauntering up to the wall outside the auditorium. Ignoring her friend's surprised look, she wrote her name in big letters at the bottom of the list. "What's the worst that could happen?"

"I one thousand percent agree." The friend bounced up and down and smiled. As the two girls slipped away from the auditorium, making their way through the middle school crowd, she added, "I'm glad you changed your mind. We're going to have so much fun. And I promise, trying out for the play won't be embarrassing."

"It'll be fun," the girl said. "Now I just need to find a song that will help me crush Velvet."

Her friend looked at her strangely. "Crush her?"

"Take her down," the girl said with a mischievous grin. She pulled her purple hair into a messy ponytail. "Show her how bad it feels to lose out on something that's so important to her. I think I'd make an amazing Dorothy. Don't you?"

The other girl put her hand on her friend's forehead and narrowed her eyes. "Are you feeling okay?"

"Fine. Why?"

Her friend shook her head. "You just don't seem like yourself. Saying you want to take her down? It's kind of . . . mean. Is that what this is all about? Revenge? I thought we were doing this to have fun together. But are you only doing this because of her?"

"I'm doing it for me. And you think it's mean?" the girl said, laughing. "This isn't mean. It's payback."

CHAPTER ELEVEN

Sitting on the bus to school Friday morning, I resisted the urge to lay my cheek against the cool window. I'd spent all day Thursday at home, having easily convinced my dad I was sick. It wasn't entirely a lie—I had set my alarm to go off every fifteen minutes on Wednesday night to prevent any more strange things from happening. Until I figured out what was going on, I wasn't ready to take any chances. By the time Thursday morning had come around, I could hardly pull myself out of bed. So instead of school, I had spent the whole day conked out on the couch, my mind spinning through bizarre dreams while soap operas played soundlessly in the background.

These dreams had felt a lot like my usual sick-day dreams—strange, true-to-life nightmares, really. The nasty guy from the bus had showed up, and like some sort of bus-defending hero, I'd stood up to him and told him what I thought of his nasty habits. Then I had signed up to audition for the musical. As had been the case before, when I touched the moonstone tucked in my pocket, the details of the dreams seemed to piece together with greater clarity. I guess that made sense, considering what I'd read about moonstones sometimes being dream stones.

Because I had slept all day Thursday, I didn't have much trouble staying awake Thursday night. This was a relief. I hoped it would keep the nighttime weirdness—sleepwalking, lost moments, whatever was going on—from happening. But now it had been a full week since I'd had a truly good night's sleep, and it was starting to show. I wanted to collapse on every available surface. That morning on the bus, I could see some-one's hair product rubbed into a greasy blot on the glass, which helped keep the temptation at bay.

Déjà vu struck when toenail man climbed into the bus and walked up the aisle, on a path directly toward me. I noticed he had a travel mug in his hand, the exact same kind I'd had on Monday, the day he'd clipped his talons into my drink. I shoved my hands deep inside my jacket pockets and balled them into fists. I so wished I could say something to that guy, but I was too much of a chicken to tell him off. I ducked my head as he came closer, hiding from his creepy gaze. The guy kept walking toward me, until finally he stood *right there*, in front of me, gawking. I looked up the tiniest bit, and he held the cup in front of my nose. He opened his mouth to speak, and an itsy-bitsy "sorry" came squeaking out.

"What?" I asked, looking at the mug hanging from his hand, just inches from my face.

"Sorry," he said, acting skittish and scared. "This is for you."

I gave him the look you might expect—suspicious and weirded out. "The cup? Is for me?" As if I was going to take it. The idea gave me the willies.

Toenail Man nodded, hastily set the mug on the seat next to me, and hightailed it back to the front of the bus where he exited at the next stop. I stared at the cup balanced on the seat next to me and put my hand around it to steady it as the bus went over a bumpy patch of road. I made a mental note to use some of the hand sanitizer in the lobby when I got to school— for all I knew, the guy had tainted the outside of the cup with poison or something.

Who gives a random stranger cocoa in a travel mug? I didn't even think the guy had realized his toenail had landed in my drink. But maybe he was torn up about it? Maybe he was doing a twelve-step thing with AA and needed my forgiveness? All I knew was that I might need to reconsider Will's offer to give me a ride to school, if only to avoid Toenail Man for the rest of my life.

"I had an idea for your audition song." Jonathan fell into step with me as I walked to my locker. "What about something classic? A song from *Annie* . . . or *Annie Get Your Gun*." He waggled his eyebrows. "Girl power!"

Anji trotted along behind us, crooning out, *"Anything you can do, I can do better . . ."*

I began to ask her what Jonathan was talking about when he went on. "Just hear me out. Everyone else is going to do more recent Broadway songs, or 'Over the Rainbow,' or Jennifer Hudson, Adele, or—God forbid—Taylor Swift. So you surprise everyone. Go old school. A classic." He grinned. "Brilliant, or ridic?"

I shoved my backpack into my locker and spun around. "I told you guys. I'm not auditioning."

Anji blinked, and I could see the shimmery green shadow she had slathered across her eyelids. "Okay, last I heard, you were. What did I miss?"

"No," I argued. "I think you're remembering what you want to remember. I'm not stepping on Velvet's toes. Besides, being up onstage just isn't for me."

"I told you she'd change her mind," Jonathan muttered under his breath.

"I didn't change my mind," I said. "I said I wasn't going to audition for *The Wizard of Oz* and I'm not." I'd never have the guts to go after something Velvet wanted so badly. Even if I *didn't* get a part in the play, my mere presence at the auditions would be enough to annoy her. Because the fact was I had a better singing voice than she did, and she knew it. The difference between her and me, though, is that I'd never have the nerve to get up onstage in front of all those people. Velvet loved that kind of attention. I feared it.

Anji looked annoyed. "Lucia, I don't get you."

I pulled a notebook out of my locker. "What's not to get?"

"Yesterday you were talking all big—you're going to crush Velvet, this is payback, all that." She got into my face and stared into my eyes. Both the closeness and what she was saying were making me squirm. "Why the change of heart? Did she say something to you?"

I swallowed, thinking about my sick dreams from the day

before: confronting the guy on the bus, signing up for auditions. I felt in my pocket for my moonstone, and when my fingers touched its smooth surface, the dreams rushed into my head again.

But they weren't dreams, I suddenly realized. They were memories.

"I don't feel well," I said quietly. "I think I might need another sick day."

"Another?" Anji asked, taking a step back. She crossed her arms and heaved a deep sigh while Jonathan felt my forehead. "You haven't been out sick all year. Come on, Lucia, just *talk* to us. Why are you being so weird this week?"

"But yesterday . . . ," I began, though I already knew what they were going to say.

"You seemed totally fine yesterday," Jonathan announced, a confused look splashed across his face. "Stole all my cookies at lunch, remember?"

"I did?"

He nodded. "So it kinda serves you right if you have a stomachache. You have to practice if you want to be able to eat that many cookies in one sitting. I'm a pro."

I closed my eyes. I was beginning to feel dizzy, from lack of sleep and everything else swirling around in my brain.

"Lu, you're completely freaking me out," Anji nudged me. "Look at me." She seemed extremely concerned, which made me think about how lucky I was to have two friends who honestly *cared* about me—unlike Velvet, who had kicked me when I was already down. "Do you want to go to the health office?"

"Not the health office." I sighed. It had been so long since I'd shared a secret with a friend—since the day I'd told Velvet about the kiss between me and Will. But Anji and Jonathan were different. I could trust them. I had to take the risk and trust *someone*, since it was clear I couldn't keep all of this to myself anymore. Though I knew it would be hard, I also knew it was time to come clean. "Do you guys think you could come over after school? I need your help."

The rest of the day dragged by. Each hour brought strange new surprises. I had begun to feel like an imposter in my own life— it was almost as if all my classmates were responding to someone else, someone who wasn't me.

In second period Daunte and Jake and a few of the other guys Will hung around with all the time gave me chummy high fives as I walked down the aisle to my back-row desk, and I heard them talking about me jumping off the bridge over the river with Will. At lunch Will briefly stopped by our table to say hi and offer me a ride home from school.

In gym Mariah Vandenburg was picked as one of the team captains for our soccer game. Mariah scoped out her options, but everyone knew she'd choose Velvet first. That's what you do—stack your team with friends, then nab as many quality players as you can, and finally fill out the rest of the spots with people like me. But instead of going in that order, Mariah stood on one side of the goal and announced her first choice: "Lucia."

Velvet had already started to walk up to stand next to Mariah, so she had to sheepishly step back while I walked forward and took my spot next to one of Velvet's best friends. Mariah grinned at me, waited as Tad Wilson picked Daunte, then made her next selection: "Velvet."

Later, in English, Velvet spent most of the hour alternately glaring at me and pretending to be my friend again. When Will was nearby, she made a big show of talking about the movie night she was hosting for the Chosen Ones and some of the guys in our grade that night. Velvet gave me a super-fake smile and said I could come by and hang out if I wanted to. *As if,* I thought, but said nothing.

"Hello?" Velvet snipped at me, as soon as Will's attention

was elsewhere. "I just *personally* invited you to hang out with my crew. The least you could do is answer or thank me. Just sitting there, saying nothing when someone is talking to you is kind of weird, you know." Briana laughed. Velvet shrugged and widened her eyes at me. "I'm just trying to help."

"I don't think I can make it," I said finally. But I couldn't keep myself from smiling when I let myself imagine what she would do if I actually showed up.

As the day went on, I couldn't decide if all this new attention was awful . . . or if it was actually kind of nice to finally be noticed. There was something so refreshing about the new way people were looking at me. The Lucia everyone else was responding to made me question the way I looked at myself.

Maybe I was the kind of girl who could stand up to Velvet.

Maybe I was the kind of girl who auditioned for musicals.

Maybe I was the kind of girl who could tell my mom how much she'd hurt me.

Maybe I was the kind of girl who got exactly what she wanted.

Maybe I wasn't flashy or special like Velvet—but I was Lucia Frank, and lately that was starting to feel pretty fantastic.

CHAPTER TWELVE

texted my sister before last period and asked if she would pick me and my friends up and drive us to our house after school. I was surprised when Romy said yes. She was even nice to us in the car—especially when she heard Anji and I were going to audition for the musical. She seemed super excited to help us figure out our audition songs and gave us a bunch of pointers for looking confident up onstage. She told us it was a little-known secret that the musical director *loved* Disney movies, especially *The Little Mermaid*, and told us he would go nuts if someone sang one of the songs from a classic Disney film. Anji seemed doubtful, but Romy promised she was telling the truth, and I believed her for the first time in a while. It was really nice to see the sister I remembered from before the divorce making a guest appearance.

As soon as we got to my house, my friends and I hid out in my room, eating Doritos. We didn't have long before Anji would have to go home for family night, so I knew I couldn't stall if I wanted their help. "Okay, so here's the thing . . ." I took a deep breath and closed my eyes. "I'm pretty sure something really weird happened to me on the night of the eclipse." I pulled my legs up against my chest and propped my chin on my knees. "When I didn't come back to the roof at Velvet's house on my birthday, it was actually because something happened. And since then, a lot *more* strange somethings have been happening."

"Like what?" Anji asked casually.

I felt my cheeks flush. What I was about to tell them sounded so stupid and crazy outside my own head. It sounded impossible *inside* my head too. I stuffed a few chips in my mouth then finally began, "So that night, I got lost when I was trying to find my way back from the bathroom. The eclipse was about to start, and I was alone on this other part of Velvet's roof trying to figure out how to get back to you guys. I don't exactly know what happened, but I was walking and all of a sudden I . . . collapsed or something. When I woke up again, the eclipse was over and Velvet was with me. She was saying all these things to me that didn't make any sense." I took a breath and shook my head. "But I had this dream while I was out—a dream that, afterward, I realized might have actually been kind of real. And I've been having more dreams like it. But I'm pretty sure they're not only dreams. I think they're things that are actually happening, but I don't remember."

I looked up at my friends. I knew I wasn't making any sense, but they weren't laughing at me or looking at me like I was crazy. They both just looked curious and a little confused. I took a deep breath and went on, trying to explain myself better. "Here's the thing: Ever since my birthday, people have been telling me about things I've said and done—when I was pretty sure I was asleep—that seem totally unlike me. When I wake up, I get brief flashes of memories, but they're those fuzzy-edged memories you have when you wake up. Like dreams you can sort of remember, if you really try hard, you know?"

My friends just stared back at me. They didn't know. In their silence the only sound was the rustle of the chip bag. "Like amnesia?" Jonathan asked finally. "You're forgetting things?"

I sighed. "No, I don't think so. But I don't know. All I know is that people have been acting really differently toward me since the night of Velvet's party. People keep telling me about things

I've done that sound really fun! And my hair!" I grabbed at the ends of my hair and tugged, as if pulling it would make it pop off like a wig. "I woke up one morning with purple hair, and I seriously don't remember dyeing it." I flopped back onto my bed and closed my eyes. "And you know how people are talking about me hanging out with Will and his friends at the river? Don't remember that, either." I told them about my wet sneakers, and how I'd stayed home sick the day before and couldn't remember signing up for the fall musical auditions, and my weird dream about yelling at the kooky bus guy and how he gave me a new travel mug that morning. "Even though I don't actually remember doing any of these things, it's clear that—somehow—I am. It's almost like I'm living a secret double life. Like there are two of me or something."

Anji nodded solemnly. "You know this sounds strange, yes?"

"It sounds impossible. I know."

"Okay." She chewed on her lower lip. "So what happened that night at Velvet's party? When you collapsed or whatever."

"No clue," I said. "I thought I heard someone behind me, but I might have imagined that. It's like I just fell asleep and totally missed the eclipse."

"What's the last thing you remember before you blacked out?" Jonathan asked.

"I was trying to get back to you guys." I felt myself flush. "And I was thinking about all the things I would wish for during the eclipse."

"Whoa." Jonathan's eyes widened. "What did you wish for?"

"I didn't wish to fall asleep during the eclipse," I said, avoiding the question. "The wishes don't matter. What I'm worried about is what could be happening. Why does it seem like I'm doing all this strange stuff, but I don't remember doing it?"

Anji chewed her lip. "Do you think you've been sleepwalking, and you just don't know it?"

I shrugged. "I don't think so."

"Have you ever been a sleepwalker before?" Jonathan asked.

"Never," I said. "At least, not that I know of. Really, it doesn't seem like sleepwalking. I've done a little research, and it sounds like most sleepwalking people usually do nonsensical things, and then wake up in some random place. It's not like you're actually going about your regular-life business when you're sleepwalking. I mean, some people do normal stuff, but when I poked around online, it looked like the longest anyone's been known to sleepwalk is half an hour. I have hours of missing time. Like *all day* yesterday when I stayed home sick to sleep!"

"Why did you stay home to sleep?" Jonathan wondered.

"My mom would never let me stay home to nap. That is, like, my *dream* day."

I laughed. "The first few times any of these weird things happened were at night. I wondered if I could prevent anything else from happening if I kept myself awake all night. So to test it, I set my alarm to wake myself up every fifteen minutes on Wednesday night. But now it seems like whatever is going on can happen during the day, too. Whenever I'm asleep. Like yesterday, while I thought I was home sick, but apparently I wasn't."

"That was a good theory, though," Anji noted, rubbing her hands together. "What other theories have you come up with?"

I took a deep breath. "Honestly? I'm worried I'm going crazy. Is it possible I'm like Jekyll and Hyde?" That was as far as I'd gotten on my own. I stuck a little piece of my hair in my mouth and chewed it. Was it possible I was slowly being poisoned by my hair dye? I spit it out.

Anji jumped up suddenly and said, "What if your mom's been right all these years?"

I looked at her curiously. I had told her about my mom's magical obsessions the week before my birthday when I was explaining why it was such a big deal I'd been born during an eclipse. "You mean, what if this is something weird? Like, magical?"

"Whatever is going on seems to have started the night of the eclipse, right?" Anji said. "There has to be some connection."

"Yeah, maybe." Now that Anji had brought up the idea of magic, I reluctantly told them about how the moonstone had changed on my birthday. Then I held it out for both of them to see. Anji grabbed it from me and studied it closely.

"With the moon and everything, have you considered that maybe you're a werewolf?" Jonathan laughed, but I could tell it was just to break the tension. "But I guess that would mean you turn into a wolf for these secret outings. I ate lunch with you yesterday, and I don't remember you being furry." He squinted a little as he studied my face. He reached out and tipped my chin back. "Is that a small shadow of a beard I see?"

"I'm not a werewolf," I said, tossing my slipper at him.

It felt good to open up to them, but I was also a little worried—deep down—that somehow voicing my secrets aloud might change things. Of course I wanted to figure out what was happening to me, and why. I worried that I was losing control of my own life. But at the same time, I wondered if it was wrong that I liked some of the side effects of my forgotten moments? The way Will was acting toward me and how we were becoming friends again; the way I was starting to feel like something more than a footstool to Velvet; how refreshing it felt to be noticed.

"I really am concerned I'm going crazy," I admitted. Then I added quietly, "But, you guys, the most messed up thing is that I'm sort of enjoying the way people have been acting around me this week." I groaned. "I hate that my life feels so off schedule. You know I hate veering off plan. I didn't mean to sign up for auditions. I didn't mean to start hanging out with Will again. I never would have dared to dye my hair purple. Of course I *want* those things . . ." I trailed off, leaving the rest unspoken. The part where I added *but I never would have the guts to do them.*

They both nodded solemnly, saying nothing for a few minutes. I could tell they were taking it all in, trying to figure out how to deal with me. Just like I'd been doing for the past week.

"What does it feel like when you wake up after one of these dreams?" Anji asked, cupping the moonstone in her palm.

"It feels like it always does after you wake up from a super-weird dream," I said. "I remember little snatches of events and conversations, but nothing that comes together as a full memory." I told them sometimes I could remember specific things, like the way I'd tasted cookies when I woke up the morning after I'd gone to the river with Will. "I am super tired, but I guess that's because it seems like I haven't really been sleeping. Whenever I'm *supposed* to be sleeping, I'm apparently going out and doing stuff instead. So I guess my body hasn't really had a full night's sleep in a week?"

Jonathan asked, "Why do you think this is happening?"

"I don't know," I said, feeling hopeless. "I can't explain any of it, and it's scary, actually, not having control over little snippets of your life. That's where you guys come in."

"I'm glad you told us," Anji said. She heaved a sigh. "I can't believe you were keeping this to yourself, Lucia. I don't know what Velvet did to you to make you not trust people, but you have to learn to lean on your friends again. That's what we're here for."

"I know," I said with a smile. "Thank you. I really need a friend right now."

"You have two!" Jonathan said, gesturing wildly at himself and Anji. "One, two!"

I laughed and felt some of the fear begin to melt away. I had told them everything, and nothing terrible had happened. "So . . . will you guys help me?"

"Call me Nate the Great!" Jonathan said, pointing his finger in the air. "Jigsaw Jones! Hardy Boy!"

"I'm not calling you any of those things," Anji said drily.

"If there's a mystery to solve, I'm your guy!" Jonathan cheered.

"Yeah, we'll see about that," Anji laughed. "If you're going to solve this mystery the way Jigsaw Jones or Nate the Great would, maybe you should start hunting for some sort of code to crack. Or a magical coin."

Jonathan pulled his eyebrows together. "A magical coin, eh?"

Anji and I both broke into a fit of giggles.

He held up his hand. "Don't laugh . . . you may be onto something."

We laughed even harder. He held out his hand for the moonstone. "What about this? It seems connected somehow. It's like a clue, yes?"

I agreed and told them what I'd learned about moonstones. Jonathan took the stone and turned it over and over in his palm. He gave Anji a pointed look and said, "Never diss the magic coin. Which, in this case, is actually a magic stone. Maybe. This is definitely a thread we should follow." He glanced up. "Do you have a microscope?"

"Why?" I asked. "And no."

"We should get a closer look at it," he said. "I have a micro-scope at home. I could take it home with me and see if there's anything weird?"

"Umm . . ." It made me a little nervous to think about giving up my moonstone, even if it was only for a short while. What if something terrible happened to it . . . or to me? What if he lost it? But I didn't want Jonathan to think I didn't trust him.

"I'll bring it back first thing tomorrow." He smiled. "Please? We have to track every lead, yes?"

"Let me think about it for a little bit," I said sheepishly. Eager to change the subject, I said, "The other thing is, my mom has this old friend who's really into dreams and stuff. Suze. She's kind of odd, but . . . I don't know. Maybe I should talk to a doctor first."

"I definitely think it would be worth talking to your mom's friend," Anji blurted out.

"But everything my mom believes in is stupid," I said, feel-ing only a little bit bad for being so blunt.

Anji shook her head. "That's not true. I don't think you can dismiss it without considering the possibility that something magical could be going on. There's no reason *not* to talk to this lady and see if she can give you any interesting information, yeah?"

"Yeah," Jonathan agreed.

"You both think I should meet with her?" I scanned their faces. They nodded. "I have to admit, as dumb as my mom's magic monkey business is, I have a weird feeling about all of this."

"Do you think this Suze chick might be able to help?" Jonathan wondered. "And have you tried talking to your mom about what's been going on? She seems like the perfect person to talk to, since she's all into this stuff."

"I haven't told my mom anything other than mentioning the weird dreams," I admitted. I didn't tell them I hadn't shared *anything* with my mom lately, that I wasn't about to confide in her unless it was absolutely necessary. "I know she'll freak out and tell my dad, and that's the last thing he needs to deal with." My heart was racing. "Do you think there's something seriously wrong with me?"

Anji wrapped an arm around me. "I don't know." She leaned her head against mine. It felt so good to have other people who knew.

Jonathan smiled reassuringly. "I am glad you told us, so you're not worrying about this by yourself."

"I wish you had trusted us enough to tell us sooner," Anji added.

Jonathan went over to my desk and opened the laptop. "Mind if I do a little browsing online?"

"Feel free," I said. "I've searched on everything that I thought could be even a little bit connected. I hit a dead end."

Jonathan poked around online for a while. While he searched, I pulled out a few of the books my mom had given me for my birthdays. Anji and I read about witchy magic and paranormal activity and hauntings. None of it seemed at all connected, except the moonstone bits I'd already read, and there wasn't much in that section that seemed relevant.

"This book is mostly about horoscopes and astrological signs," Anji said, pawing through a slim book. "Were you born on a cusp?"

"I don't think so," I said.

"What's a cusp?" Jonathan asked. "Cusp makes me think of custard, which makes me think of dessert. Got anything good in the kitchen, Lucia?"

"Lucky Charms?" I offered. "Help yourself. Cupboard next to the fridge."

Jonathan dashed downstairs and returned a minute later

with an overflowing bowl of Lucky Charms. "Your dad's down there," he said. "Cool guy. He says hi, and seemed surprised that you have friends over. Not bad surprised, just surprised."

"He's home?"

"Yeah," Jonathan slurred through a mouthful of colored marshmallows. "He's watching TV."

"Of course he is," I muttered. "That's all he does, ever since my mom left. I wish I could figure out some way to get him to go out with friends or something again. He needs to move on."

"Have you suggested that he go out?" Anji asked. "He might just need a nudge."

I shook my head. "No. I don't want to hurt his feelings and tell him I think he's kind of a loser."

She rolled her eyes. "Of course you don't. But you're *thinking* it? That's almost worse. Why don't you just try being honest?"

"The truth hurts," I said.

Jonathan took another huge bite of his cereal, slopping a bit of milk onto my rug. "Sorry," he said. "Hey, you never told me what a cusp is, Anj."

"Oh, right," she said, glancing up from the book she was paging through. "If someone's born on a cusp, it means they're born on one of the days that kind of falls between two astrological signs. Sometimes, if you're born on a cusp it sort of splits your personality in two. For example, I'm just reading about people born between August nineteenth and August twenty-fourth. They're on the Leo-Virgo cusp. So a lot of times they can be either super-duper outgoing, or extra secretive. It says here that Leo-Virgo cusps are really good at figuring out when to speak up and when to keep quiet." She looked at me. "It also says people born on the Leo-Virgo cusp need to let others into their lives to share their feelings. Hiding away is a bad thing . . . sound like anyone we know? A certain someone who kept all these weird happenings to herself? Hmm?"

"Me?" I asked. "I wasn't born in August. My birthday was last week. I'm a Libra, the most boring sign ever. We're all about balance. We like harmony, and peace, and keeping other people happy. We're also, apparently, very charming." I grinned at her.

Anji nodded. "But listen to this. It's kind of interesting: 'This cusp is influenced by Leo's flair for the dramatic and Virgo's lack of sociability. When the strengths of both signs come together—combining the power of two signs—these individuals will really discover their true abilities.'"

"I'm still not an August baby," I reminded her.

"The power of two," Anji said, looking up from the book. "Bringing together two halves of your personality . . . it's kind of what's happening to you, isn't it? You're usually all quiet and shy and secretive, but in these dreams you've been having—or whatever is happening—you're acting like a different person. It's almost like another side of your personality is coming out, yes?"

"Maybe," I said. Jonathan wiggled his eyebrows.

"Okay, here's what we know so far," Anji said, ticking things off on her fingers. "You have a changed moonstone, have been having weird dreams about things you kind of wish you had the guts to do, odd things are happening when you think you're asleep . . . and it all started on the night of the eclipse. Which was also the night of your birthday."

"Yep."

She asked, "It's all connected somehow, don't you think?"

"I think it must be," I agreed. "So what do the moonstone, my birthday, the eclipse, and my dreams all have to do with one another?"

Neither of them said anything. Finally, Jonathan shrugged and said, "No clue. Jigsaw Jones and Nate the Great can only take me so far. And unless you give me the moonstone for the night, we're kinda stuck on that lead."

"We've got to go see this Suze chick," Anji said finally. "We're stuck. There's no rational way to explain any of this, so I think our only choice is to talk to one of the people you call crazy."

"She's not crazy," I said. "Just a little unusual. Floaty."

"Whatever she is, she's a lead. You call her, and we'll go with you to talk to her," Anji instructed.

"Aye, aye, Captain." I saluted her. For once I was happy to have someone else take the lead.

"In the meantime," she said, "we have to figure out how you're going to get some sleep. We need to keep your sleepy-time wanderings to a minimum."

I knew she was right, but still a part of me was curious about what else might happen if I did let myself fall asleep. What would happen if I just let go?

"What if Anji spent the night?" Jonathan suggested. "She could keep an eye on you if you went to sleep. You could take turns, being Lucia lookout. And hey, if Anji's here to protect you, you wouldn't need your moonstone, right?"

"I wouldn't ask you to do that," I said, glancing at Anji and ignoring Jonathan's question.

"You wouldn't. But you should," she said, fixing me with a stern look. "That's what friends are for. Maybe that's not

147

the way your friendship with Velvet worked, but that's how it works with me. True friendships are built through trust and helping each other."

"Okay, then," I said, relief washing over me. "Will you stay over?"

Anji cringed. She looked sheepish and said, "Um, but tonight is family night. I know my parents won't let me. How about tomorrow?"

"I can stay for a while tonight," Jonathan offered. "No family night for me. My mom's working late. I'm guessing your dad wouldn't be super psyched about me staying over, but I can definitely stick around for a while. We can hang out and maybe you can nap or something while I'm here to watch over you?"

We all cracked up when he said that. The thought of napping while Jonathan sat over me and kept watch seemed seriously creepy. But a nap was really appealing, and I was happy that he was willing to hang out even without Anji being around. I wondered if *Anji* was okay with us spending time without her—Velvet would have been insanely jealous if she were in the same position. "Is that okay with you?" I asked her. "If the two of us hang out without you?"

"Of course!" Anji said without a moment's pause. "I think that's a great idea."

"Then, yeah," I said. "Sounds good."

"I promise I'll figure out some way to convince my parents to let me stay over tomorrow night," Anji vowed. "This is going to be super fun. Me, you, and nighttime Lu!"

CHAPTER THIRTEEN

When Anji left, Jonathan dragged a chair in front of my bedroom door and folded his arms across his chest like some kind of scrawny bodyguard. Then he told me that I could take a nap while he watched a movie or listened to music on his phone.

"There's no way I'm going to sleep with you staring at me. That's too weird. It's nice just having someone to hang out with. The best thing you can do is keep me awake. I'm exhausted."

Jonathan suggested that, instead of hanging out in my room where my pillow was surely calling to me, we could hang out downstairs and find something to eat. It sounded like a good idea to me, and I knew we had a frozen pizza, so we made our way to the kitchen. Just as the oven timer went off, Dad wandered in. He looked excited to have someone other than Romy and me around the house (especially since my sister was almost always locked away in her room). I kept trying to pull Jonathan away, to drag him and our pizza back to my room to avoid a night spent yammering with my dad, but Jonathan didn't seem to mind him being there.

"So Lucia tells me you're an accountant?" Jonathan said, making it sound like my dad's job was the most exciting career choice ever. He settled in at the counter, looking ready for a nice, long chat. "How is that?"

"How *is* that?" Dad repeated, scratching his slightly stubbly chin. "Not thrilling, I can tell you that much." He chuckled. "But it's not awful. My boss is the pits, and I'd give anything to have one day of my life where I *don't* look at the computer, but it's better than no job at all. How's that for an answer?"

"Well said, Mr. Frank," Jonathan said politely, with a nod.

I gave him a funny look. "What are you doing?" I whispered when my dad opened the fridge to get out some milk for us.

"Making conversation," Jonathan said.

"About my dad's job?" I asked, lifting my eyebrows.

"What else do I talk to him about?" he asked. "I'm not exactly a dad expert. The only thing my own dad ever talks to me about is sports—which I don't play *or* watch—and his job, if he talks to me at all. If I'm not careful, I'll get nervous and accidentally spill everything I know about *you know what*." He wiggled his eyebrows and made himself look like a zombie. I guessed he was talking about my nighttime wanderings, but I'm not sure what zombies had to do with it.

My dad returned to the counter and poured two tall glasses of milk. He plunked them down in front of us. In a weird voice I'd never heard before, Jonathan asked, "So how about those fierce Giants, Mr. Frank?"

"Fierce giants?" my dad asked, looking at me as though I might be able to offer him an explanation. "Is that a book you're reading? Or a TV show?"

I laughed out loud—it was impossible not to.

"Oh." Jonathan's cheeks flushed. "Are you more of a Jets guy?" That's when my dad started laughing too. "What's funny? Did you move to New York from another state? Are you a Seahawks fan? Patriots? One of those cheeseheads who don't wear shirts in the cold?" I'd never seen Jonathan flustered before. Slightly uncomfortable or shy, sure. But at the moment, my friend who always knew just what to say to lighten the mood seemed completely at a loss. "Help me out here, people. Those are the only football teams I know."

"I can honestly say I don't know the first thing about football," my dad said. "Or baseball. Or basketball, for that matter. I follow a little soccer, but mostly I'm a movie-and-books kind of guy."

Jonathan looked relieved. "Me too!"

"Do you have a favorite book?" my dad asked, leaning against the counter.

"A few," Jonathan said eagerly. "I've always been a big Roald Dahl fan. And Harry Potter, obviously—but my dad says I'm too old for fantasy. I'm just getting into Carl Hiaasen. He's funny."

"You're never too old for fantasy," my dad said, shaking his head. "But I do love Carl Hiaasen."

"Really?" Jonathan asked, incredulous. "You've heard of him?"

"Of course."

"Maybe you guys should start a book club," I interrupted, only slightly kidding.

"I can't believe you've read Carl Hiaasen," Jonathan muttered. "My dad only reads self-help books. Not that they really help him."

My dad laughed. "I'd be happy to talk with you about books anytime, Jonathan."

"Seriously?" Jonathan looked like someone had just offered him an entire chocolate cake—with sprinkles and a side of ice cream.

"It would be my pleasure." Dad handed each of us a cookie, then popped one into his own mouth before heading for the kitchen door. "Let me know if you guys need anything else, all right? Jonathan, I can give you a ride home whenever you need to go. But stay as long as you like. I'll be in the living room watching some TV."

When we got back up to my bedroom, Jonathan said, "Your dad is so awesome, Lucia."

"Yeah," I agreed. "He's not bad."

"No, seriously. If I had a dad like that . . ." He trailed off.

"I've heard you talk about your dad a little bit," I said, hoping I wasn't treading into uncomfortable territory. I knew if I were in his shoes, I wouldn't want anyone asking any questions about my mom. "But I don't know much."

Jonathan shrugged and pushed his hair back from his face. "I don't usually talk about this with Anji much anymore, since she doesn't really get it. Her family is so perfect that I think it's hard for her to understand. She tries, but it can be hard for someone in a really good place to realize how far the pieces of your life

154

fly when a family splits up. But you get it. Right?" I nodded, realizing this was one of the first conversations Jonathan and I had ever had without Anji around. "I was nine when my dad left. We got along okay when I was little, but the older I got, the more obvious it became that he and I were seriously different. I love music and books and drawing, and he likes sports and money . . . and himself."

"Come on, you must have a few things in common," I said, laughing. Leave it to Jonathan to make even a downer conversation somewhat funny.

"I honestly have no idea." Jonathan frowned. "He mostly stopped showing up for his weekends a couple years ago. Lots of excuses and apologies. We hardly talk at all."

"Are you serious? Do you ever tell him how you feel?"

"Lots of times. He'll make an effort for a while, but then it's like he forgets we ever had the conversation. I'm not going to stop trying, though." Jonathan grabbed my moonstone off the bedside table and rolled it around in his palm while he talked. I wondered if it offered him the same calming effect it did me. "I don't ever want to give up on our relationship and regret it later."

"That has to be hard."

"It's *very* hard. Whenever we do hang out, he mostly lectures me and tries to convert me into a football fan. For a little while, I tried to be the kid he wanted me to be—but then I realized it wasn't worth changing who I am just to make him happy." He stared at the stone, rubbing his thumb along the deep black core. "It's okay. My mom is great and we do fine, just the two of us. I wish she didn't have to work so much, but she got a second job so she doesn't have to take as much money from my dad. She said his money is rotten."

"Sheesh, Jonathan." I blinked. I thought about how different Jonathan's situation was from my own. Sure, my parents were divorced, but Mom obviously still cared, and she made a serious effort to stay close and connected. I wondered if, over time, she would begin to distance herself the way Jonathan's dad had? Deep down, I knew the answer was no. As mad as I was at her for everything that had happened with our family, I knew she would never stop wanting to spend time with me.

"Sheesh is a pretty good word for it," Jonathan said lightly. "So that's why I like your dad. He's so nice. And it's fun talking to him."

"You can come over and hang out with him whenever you like," I offered. *"Mi casa es su casa."*

156

"Thanks. I'll definitely take you up on that. Nice job with your Spanish vocab, by the way." Jonathan glanced at my alarm clock and then stood up. "I'm really sorry, but I should probably get home. Are you going to be okay here tonight?" He tossed me my moonstone, adding, "I won't take that tonight, since I'm leaving you alone." I caught it and stuffed it inside my pocket.

"I'll be fine," I told him. "In fact, as soon as you leave, I'm gonna head over to Velvet's house for that movie night she's doing with the Chosen Ones and Will and his friends. They can keep me occupied."

Jonathan stared at me without saying anything. After a beat he swallowed and said, "For real?"

"Of course not for real!" I threw my stuffed elephant at him. It bopped him on the head then bounced back onto the bed. "I'm just going to try to stay up as long as I can, then I guess I'll hope for the best?"

"I have an idea," Jonathan said, scampering over to my door. "How about I rig something up so if you try to leave this room, you'll wake up?" He made sure my door was shut tight, then proceeded to stack a whole bunch of things—books, shoes, a basket filled with tubes of lip gloss—in a tippy-looking stack. "There," he said, crab-walking back across the room to inspect his handiwork from afar. "If you try to get through that door, it will all fall and make a giant mess."

"How are you going to get out?"

"Right. That is a fair question." He pulled his eyebrows together, then scuttled back over to the stack and carved a small path through the barricade. "I'll squeeze through here when I leave. If you're sleepwalking, there's no way you'll be in the right mind to get through this maze without knocking something over, right?"

"I dunno," I said. "I don't know how this magic—or whatever it is—works. And what if I have to go to the bathroom?"

"What time is your scheduled evening toilet break?" Jonathan asked seriously.

"Not that again!" I said, and pelted him with a pillow. "I do *not* plan bathroom breaks. I try to plan as much stuff as I can since almost all of life's little surprises are giant bummers—but I don't go that far."

"I know." He laughed. "And I get it—about life's surprises, I mean."

"Yeah," I said, nodding. "Thanks for telling me about your dad."

"Of course. We're friends, right?" He saluted me and said,

"Later, Lucia. Let me know how it goes tonight."

As soon as he was gone, I lay down on my bed and looked up at my ceiling. There were still a few glow-in-the-dark stars stuck in one corner of the room, remnants of a package Will and I had split between us a few summers before.

Will. Once again I wondered how different everything might have been if it hadn't been for that dumb kiss and Velvet's lies. Or would it? Who could know for sure what might have happened over the summer or once middle school started? So much was changing, and it was impossible to predict things I couldn't control. One thing I did know for sure was that I should have told Velvet she had been a bad friend. I should have stood up for myself.

At least I had gotten to know Jonathan and Anji because of all that had happened. Eventually, maybe, I would be as close to them as I had once been with both Velvet and Will. If I were one to believe in silver linings, I'd say that was the one good thing that had come from Velvet's betrayal: my growing friendship with Anji and Jonathan. When she cast me aside, they were there to rescue me. And I was pretty sure the best was yet to come.

OUT OF THE SHADOWS

The moment the girl arrived at the party, something in her began to buzz. A little spark was daring her to live in the moment. The time had come to show the other girl she wasn't afraid of her anymore. She walked around the giant lion and passed by the wall of antiques, crossing through to the dining room. There were empty salad bowls scattered across the table, waiting for someone to whisk them away. Inside the living room a dozen girls were doing their nails. The tangy sharpness of nail polish rose up around them like a shield. She stepped through it.

As the girl stood surveying the party from the fringes, one of the Chosen Ones hopped up and air-kissed her—as though they had been expecting her all along. "Hi!" The other girl giggled, holding her hands delicately in the air to keep her polish from smudging. "I can't believe you actually came. I'm glad you did, but . . . she's definitely going to be surprised!" She pulled the girl's arm with her glossy-nailed hand. "Want me to do your nails?"

The girl shrugged off her leather jacket and settled in on the plush carpet. Unlike the first time she'd been in this house, the girl now had nothing to lose and she was no longer a fool.

"I love your hair." A hand reached out to touch a strand of hair that came down over the girl's face. "It's such a pretty color. I wish I had the nerve to do something like that. My parents would kill me." Someone else carefully painted the girl's nails with a dark polish they had selected to match her purplish hair.

Suddenly the hostess danced into the room and crooned, "The boys are here!" Everyone squealed, and the girl's nails were forgotten. She was left with one hand painted a deep purple, the other naked.

As everyone raced out of the room, the girl approached the hostess. The two stared at each other for a moment. "You came."

"You invited me."

"I didn't mean it."

The girl shrugged, unconcerned.

"When are you going to realize you're not a part of my world anymore? Stop trying."

"I can honestly say I don't want to be a part of it." The girl considered all the things she'd wished she had said before now. How could she get closure? Finally, she said, "I just need to know: Do you ever feel bad about what you did? You ruined everything."

"Feel bad? You still don't get it, do you?" The other girl smiled.

"You ruined things yourself. Some people make things happen, others let things happen."

"Why did you lie?"

"If he meant that much to you, he had to be worth it."

The girl looked her old friend straight in the eye and said, "I hope it all falls apart and you're left with nothing."

CHAPTER FOURTEEN

woke with a start, glanced at my clock, and sat up in a panic—nine o'clock. Morning, or still night? *Please,* I silently begged. *Please still be night.*

But Jonathan hadn't left until nine the night before, and I could see through the window that the sky was bright and sunny, one of those beautiful fall days that draws the entire world outside. I was tangled up in my covers, still fully dressed. I groaned and then looked hopefully at the booby traps in front of my bedroom door. My room was a complete disaster—stuff scattered everywhere. It had never been such a mess. Clearly Jonathan's trap hadn't kept me from leaving in the night. I crawled out of bed and set to work picking everything up and stacking it in piles, while thinking the same thing over and over: It happened again.

I felt for my moonstone and found it was still tucked securely in my pocket. When I rubbed it, a stream of images came flooding into my mind: the blurry streak of streetlights and car headlights, my sister at the wheel, Velvet's face up close. The moonstone had to be involved in all of this. To deny it was foolish. I'd been a fool about too many things for far too long.

As soon as I was dressed, I went out into the hall and stood outside my sister's door. Romy was organizing her closet. Ever since Mom left—and abandoned her lawyer's salary—things had been tighter than usual on the cash front. The divorce had forced us all to get creative, and I was endlessly fascinated by Romy's ability to keep herself looking good without the no-limit credit cards that so many other kids in our school seemed to have access to.

I stood in the door and watched her for a few minutes. When she finally noticed me, she looked up and smiled. "Hey," she said, not unfriendly. "Still glad you went?" I nodded vaguely, hoping she'd keep talking and give me a clue about what had happened in the night. Romy twisted her hair into a deliberately messy heap that looked like a giant cinnamon bun atop her head. "Can I ask you something?"

"Sure," I said.

"Do you have a crush on Will? Is that why you went over there? I saw the fall-out between you and Velvet when you got back from Sweden. Did something happen because he's hanging out with Velvet now?"

"No," I said honestly. "Will and I are just friends. That's all." *Are* friends . . . or *were*? I wasn't really certain where things stood.

"You sure?"

"That I don't have a crush on Will? I'm sure." I picked at my thumbnail. My eyes bugged out when I saw that my nails were polished a deep, lustrous purple. I held up the other hand and noticed that those nails were unpainted. "Romy?" I said timidly. "If I tell you something crazy, do you promise not to laugh?"

An hour later I had told Romy everything. It felt so good to get it off my chest again. I made her promise not to tell Dad—yet. She agreed, but only if I promised to talk to Suze as soon as I could. "As much as I think Mom and her friends are full of crap, you have to talk to an adult. This is weird, Lulu. Scary."

"I know," I said, thinking that what was happening was much more than just weird and scary. It was also thrilling.

"I will talk to Suze. And Anji's going to sleep over tonight to keep an eye on me."

"That's a good idea. I'll help too, if you need me. I was supposed to go over to Alaina's tonight, but I can stay home if you want." Romy pulled me into a hug. "You're going to be okay." I buried my nose in her shoulder, breathing in her soothing lavender body spray and thinking about how she used to take care of me when I'd skinned my knee or someone had said something mean to me. She murmured into my hair, "We're gonna be okay. Right?"

I wasn't sure if she was reassuring me, or if she was looking for me to reassure her. Either way, I nodded. It felt good to have my sister back.

Feeling a little lighter and a lot hungrier, I went downstairs to grab some breakfast. When I asked my dad about having a sleepover with Anji, he was totally on board. In fact, he got all quiet and said, "Maybe I should see if Greg can come over for a few beers? You and Romy are putting me to shame with your exciting social lives."

"Romy puts us all to shame," I said, laughing. "But yeah, I think you should *definitely* call Greg. Anji and I will stay out of your way. We won't butt in on man time."

He rubbed his unshaven face, then looked down at his sweats and pit-stained T-shirt. "Maybe change?"

I laughed. "That might be a good idea too."

His face brightened. "You know what? I'm going to check with David and Jeff, too. Get the poker gang back together."

"Poker gang?"

"We played a little back in the day. I took more money from those guys than I ought to admit." He chuckled. "Your mom was never a poker fan. Always said gambling encouraged too much competition among friends." He put his hands on his hips and jutted out his chin. "But your mom isn't here, so I guess it doesn't really matter what she thinks of poker anymore, does it?"

"Whoa," I said, laughing. "Who took my dad and replaced him with a rebel?"

"And you know what? I'm not shaving. I'm growing this beard until it dangles in my coffee. She doesn't own my hair anymore, either."

"Mom never owned your hair." Gently I added, "You just let her tell you what you could and couldn't do. Time to stop now, right?"

"As long as I'm on a roll, I think I'll get Mickey D's for lunch. A Big Mac *and* fries. So there."

My dad, Romy, and I had more fun that day than we'd had in months. We ate lunch at McDonald's, went for ice cream, then stopped to toss a Frisbee back and forth at the park. We didn't talk about Mom, and it felt good to see my dad look truly happy again for the first time in months.

I told Dad I was sort of considering auditioning for the school musical, and he confessed that he was thinking of looking for a new job. He had grown bored of spreadsheets and a boss who made him feel awful every day. Romy actually looked interested in the conversation throughout most of the afternoon, which was really saying something. It was one of the best Saturdays I'd had in a long time, and I had a good feeling that things were shifting for all of us.

When Anji got to my house that night, she and I hid out in my room while Dad and his friends laughed over their game of poker in the kitchen. All night long I kept thinking about how different it was hanging out with Anji than it ever had been with Velvet. I felt like I could act more like my real self with her, that I could be a little like the Lucia I'd always been around Will. I didn't have to worry about whether I sounded too babyish or worry that she would yell at me for not *getting it*. I'd never understood what *it* was, but Velvet had often rolled her eyes and said I didn't "get it" when she was telling me stories. The two of them seemed so similar in so many ways—outgoing and showy, fearless leaders of their pack—but they were total opposites where it mattered most.

Over the past few months I'd come to realize that with Velvet, everything had always been about her. She'd always taken control of the conversation. Now that I could see how it was supposed to work with a girlfriend, I realized Velvet probably knew very little about me. She had always spent so much time complaining about her parents, or worrying about how to get back at somebody who had said something wrong to her, or planning what we were going to do next, that she'd never asked me much of anything. I'd never really considered talking about myself when we were together. Her life had always seemed so much more interesting. It frustrated me to think that my so-called best friend had made me feel like I was worthless.

With Anji, things were more even. We snuck down to the kitchen to get some snacks, and after, Anji told me about her grandparents in India who were coming to visit for a month. Their visits always made Anji's mom cry because she missed her extended family. I told her a little bit about Johanna and my mom and what it had been like visiting them in Sweden this summer. After everything Jonathan had told me about his dad the night before, it wasn't as scary letting her in, somehow.

Giggling, Anji confessed that she had the tiniest crush on Daunte Adams, and I finally told her about that awful kiss with Will and what had happened with Velvet when I came home from my summer away. She squealed when she realized that meant I'd actually *kissed* someone, and then she tried to get me to answer a million questions. I told her I couldn't even talk about it, since the whole thing had been so wrong. "Will's just a friend," I said with certainty. "It was a dumb thing to do, since we'll never be anything more than that. That's why it's so weird that Velvet hates when he talks to me. I have no interest in stealing him as a boyfriend."

"Oh my gosh!" Anji said, bouncing up and down on my bed. "She's jealous. That's why she wants to set you up with Jeremy Hiller, and why she's been acting mean to you. She thinks Will is going to ditch her for you—she's threatened! She probably knows he likes you better than he'll ever like her, and that's killing her."

"Really?" I asked. "You think *Velvet* is jealous of *me*?"

Anji nodded. "Totally. She probably thinks Will is going to pick you over her, and she's trying to make sure Will picks her.

I bet she figured if you and Will were still friends, she'd have to share him with you."

"Velvet doesn't share," I said.

"Exactly." Anji paused, chewing at her lower lip. Her smile faltered. "I don't want to be anything like Velvet Mills, obviously, but sometimes I worry we're sort of alike."

"You are *not* alike," I insisted. "Not in any of the ways it matters, anyway."

"I'm not popular, or super rich, or mean to people just for fun—but in the same way Velvet worries about Will ditching her for you, I definitely get nervous you'll realize you made a mistake when you picked me as a friend." She hugged her knees to her chest.

"That would never happen," I assured her.

She grinned. "I hope not."

A bubble of guilt boiled in my stomach when I thought about what it seemed had happened the night before. First thing this morning Anji had texted to ask me if anything weird had happened in the night. I don't know what made me lie, but I said no. I knew I should tell her about where I'd gone and not keep any more secrets from her. But I didn't want to hurt her feelings. If she knew I'd gone to Velvet's movie night, it would make her worry even more. It was easier to lie.

After a long pause Anji surprised me by saying, "You're different from me and Velvet, Lucia. You have this quiet confidence. I don't think you realize it. But you do."

"Quiet confidence?" I giggled.

"Your life seems all planned out, and you have these . . . convictions," Anji said. "Like you just know who you are."

My eyes widened. "That is so not true. I told you about how I'd made wishes on the night of the eclipse, right?" Anji nodded and I went on. "So there are a ton of things I wish I could change about myself, and those are the things I wished for that night. I mean, I wish I could fix everything with Will, obviously."

"It seems like you're kind of doing that," Anji said. "Since Velvet's party, things have been more normal between you two again, right?"

"Maybe. But only because it seems like I've been doing or saying stuff when I think I'm asleep," I pointed out. "I also wished I had the guts to let my mom and Velvet know how much they've both hurt me. The way Velvet just dropped me last summer—it was awful. And my mom leaving really killed me. I feel like she sort of sprung it on us and didn't even think about how her sudden move halfway across the world was going to affect the rest of us. And it seems like she's fitting into her new life so perfectly. I wish I could tell her how much I hate that she ruined our lives to make her own life better. I know that's not fair, but it's true."

"You should tell her that," Anji said. "Seriously. She's your mom. You can't bottle that stuff up. You need her."

"I know." I sighed. It felt so good to speak my feelings aloud for once, and I realized maybe Anji was right. Maybe it was time for me to stop acting like everything was just fine. I missed the relationship I used to have with my mom. I longed for her to apologize, to explain. But she didn't even know I was waiting for that. And no one ever tried to figure out how to fix something they didn't know was broken. "It just seems like sometimes it's easier not to say anything, you know?"

Anji shook her head. "No. I don't know. I usually just say what I'm thinking, then regret it later."

"That's another thing I wished for," I said. "That I had your confidence to be truthful, and speak my mind when I'm mad about something. Like the bus guy and his gross grooming habits."

"You must have said something to him during one of your

sleeping thingies," Anji said excitedly. "Maybe that's why he brought you a new travel mug the other day!"

"Who knows." I flopped back onto my bed and groaned.

"It sounds to me like something or someone is trying to help make your wishes come true. Any other wishes? You got greedy, girl! What are we on, three already?"

"It was my birthday eclipse." I laughed. "I decided I deserved a few extras." I thought back to my last wish—bravery, just like the Cowardly Lion. "I've always been the kind of person who hides from the spotlight. But sometimes I envy people like you and Velvet. So my other wish was for bravery . . . that I could muster up the nerve to do things like try out for the play, speak up more often, just get out of my own shadow and let people know I exist, you know?"

"Another wish that's coming true," Anji mused. "Lucia, I think you have a fairy godmother or something. Someone or something wants to see your wishes granted."

"Mother Moon," I said.

"Maybe so." Anji laughed.

"I'm like a combo of all the characters in *The Wizard of Oz*. The Tin Man wants a heart, the Cowardly Lion wants courage, the Scarecrow wants a brain . . . I want all those things and more. I basically wished that I could change my life and become someone I'm not."

"You're *not* trying to be someone else," Anji said quietly. "With those wishes, you're just trying to become a different version of yourself. By wishing it, you're taking the first step to making it happen."

I thought about that for a minute. She was right. I'd often wished I could live my life a little differently. I just hadn't ever had the guts.

By eleven o'clock I was so sleepy I could hardly put together a full sentence. Anji forced me to try to fall asleep, promising she would stay awake to keep an eye on me. She sat at my desk and watched funny animal videos on YouTube to keep herself from nodding off.

Maybe it was the creep factor (having someone turn around to check on you every few minutes while you try to drift off is seriously weird), but it took me forever to fall asleep. Though I was exhausted from a week of too little sleep, I was so nervous about what might happen while Anji was on lookout that I just kept tossing and turning.

A little after midnight Anji set to work stacking up the same kind of elaborate booby traps Jonathan had put in front of the door the night before. Not long after, my bedroom door was totally blocked with noisy stuff that would clatter and smash if I tried to go anywhere. She was much better at building booby traps than Jonathan was. I smiled sleepily. "Thanks."

"Anything for you," she promised in a whisper. She settled into her sleeping bag on the floor and then reached over to take my hand in her tiny one. For the first time in months, the first time since that afternoon in the tree house with Will, I felt like someone really had my back.

I closed my eyes again. My head throbbed from the marathon of thoughts running through my mind: a great day with Dad, my improving relationship with Will, all my forgotten moments, Velvet, the upcoming auditions. So much had happened in the past week. It was as though life had flipped me upside down and inside out under a wave, and I couldn't swim fast enough to keep my head above water. I was drowning in a riptide of thoughts and emotions. Before I knew it, my exhaustion dragged me under, and I slipped into a sleep so deep and divine that nothing could wake me.

CHAPTER FIFTEEN

n the morning the stack of stuff was still exactly as Anji had left it the night before. As far as we could tell, nothing had happened in the night. Nothing moved, nothing shifted. I was both relieved and disappointed. I'd hoped to wake up to answers, to get some sort of proof or explanation that would explain what exactly happened to me during my missing moments.

Anji told me she had stayed awake until three. "Then I crashed. But nothing weird happened before I drifted off. You even snored a little."

I giggled and pulled my covers up over my face. "Really?"

"Okay, more than a little," she said, laughing along with me. "You sounded like a goat."

"No I didn't!"

"You did!" She was laughing so hard she had to gasp for air. "You were totally out." She made horrible snorting, snoring sounds, and we both laughed even harder. When she caught her breath, Anji said, "I'm sure if anything weird was going to happen, it would have happened by three, right?"

"I guess."

We went downstairs for breakfast, interrupting my dad's morning yoga. *"Namaste!"* he chirped, popping out of a clumsy Downward Dog. "Sleep well, ladies?"

"Um," Anji said, choking back a giggle. Dad was wearing his usual tank top, and I wondered if Anji would ever be able to look at him the same way again.

"Dad, can you put on a sweatshirt or something?" I asked.

Anji raced into the kitchen to hide. Once Dad had scuttled up the stairs, she told me, "My dad wears a teal bathrobe, and he has more chest hair than a gorilla. It's so much worse than a tank top. Trust me."

We both poured big bowls of cereal and sat at the kitchen table. "Why do you think strange stuff happens *some* nights, but not others?" I asked in a whisper. "Do you think nothing happened last night because you were here? Does that break the magic or something?"

"But you think you heard someone behind you on the night of the eclipse . . . ," Anji said, chewing thoughtfully. "Didn't you say you thought you heard a footstep before you fainted or whatever happened?"

I nodded. "But that could have been my imagination. It was seriously creepy up on that rooftop alone, and my mind could have been playing tricks on me."

"If there was someone else there, though, then that means you don't have to be alone for whatever's happening to you to happen. The only things that were different about last night were the expertly barricaded door and me watching over you."

Anji poked at the colored marshmallows in her bowl. Suddenly she asked, "Have there been any nights when you've been without your moonstone? Did Jonathan take it home with him on Friday? Because if nothing happened that night and you didn't have your moonstone, and nothing happened last night . . ." She trailed off.

"No," I said. "I kept it. And I had it during my sick day on Thursday. I slept with it last night. I know I had it the night of the eclipse." I thought back but couldn't remember every night over the past week. "I keep it near most nights." I tried to dredge up more memories, then suddenly remembered.

"I know I had it the night I supposedly went to the river with Will, because I'd tucked it inside my sweatshirt pocket before falling asleep on the couch. But I honestly can't remember other nights."

"Maybe you should try sleeping without it tonight? Just to be safe?"

"Yeah," I said reluctantly. But if nothing had happened last night and I *had* my moonstone, what difference would it make if I slept without it for a night? I wasn't sure I was willing to risk it. I told her, "Maybe."

After Anji went home, I opened my e-mail. My mom had sent me Suze's phone number and e-mail address earlier in the week. I'd promised Jonathan and Anji that I would call and set up a time for all of us to meet with her and talk through my situation as soon as she had time. When I opened my e-mail, I saw that I had an unread message in the e-mail chain between my mom and me. She'd sent it a few hours earlier.

Lucia, it said. *We need to talk about all of this face-to-face. Please Skype me when you're up. Mom.*

I scrolled down to read the last message I'd sent—at four in the morning. My body tensed when I read it:

Mom,

You always tell me I should talk to you about things,
but I don't think you actually want to know what
I'm thinking. I think you just say that, knowing I'll
forgive you for leaving. But here's the truth: I'm sick
of acting like everything is okay between us when it's
not. You need to know that I don't think it's fair that
you walked out on your life. I'm sorry you weren't
happy, but it was really selfish to move so far away
and start a new life. What was wrong with the life
you had? Why do you have to leave all of us to find
yourself? What did we do wrong? I don't want to
hear any of your lame excuses about soul mates and
finding your chi. Tell me the truth for once. Why did
you need to ruin my life to make yours better?

My breath caught in my throat. I had sent that e-mail. *Me.*
There, in words, were all the things I'd been thinking for the
last few months—since the family meeting when Mom had
made her big announcement—but hadn't ever said that bluntly
to anyone, except Will. I reached into my pocket and rubbed my
fingers over the moonstone. Suddenly a brilliant flash of a dream

came swimming into focus: me at the computer, typing. Nothing dramatic—just that and no more. So something *had* happened in the night. I hadn't gone anywhere, but I sure had done something.

I wasn't ready to face my mom yet, but I knew we'd have to talk soon. I'd put a lot into the e-mail, and I knew she would want to go through each of my thoughts in great detail. As sleepy and out of it as I was, I just didn't think I could face her. I quickly wrote her an e-mail back, saying that yes, we did need to talk—but could we wait a day or two so I could "collect my thoughts and have a more productive conversation"? I thought she would appreciate my mature wording.

She wrote back almost immediately and said waiting a day was fine, but that she was eager to talk to me as soon as I was ready. Then she thanked me for the e-mail, complimented me on how expressive I had been, and said she was grateful I'd finally reached out.

Huh. That was unexpected. I felt this huge weight lift off me, and for the first time in a while, I was sort of looking forward to talking to my mom.

I spent the rest of the day working with Romy on my audition song for *The Wizard of Oz*. I was starting to get really nervous about the tryouts and began to have second thoughts. But

Romy assured me I sounded great and needn't worry. She even gave me a few great tips for overcoming stage fright.

In the afternoon Dad trimmed his beard into a really awful goatee and ordered a few new shirts online with the money he had taken from his friends at poker the night before. That night Dad, Romy, and I made pizzas together. With all of us beginning to heal and move forward, it seemed like we were finding a way to fit together as a family. It was a different kind of family than we'd always been accustomed to, but it was one that might work eventually.

I sang my audition song for Romy and my dad one more time before bed. Then I took a shower and sang to myself in the mirror. I began to feel hopeful about my chances of making it into the cast, but I still hadn't decided if I was going to go through with the audition. My song was ready, but I wasn't sure *I* was ready.

That night I decided to take Anji's advice and sleep without my moonstone. I left it inside my jacket pocket downstairs so I would have it in the morning, but I knew it was safely out of reach in the night. I put my phone downstairs too, just to be safe. Before I fell asleep, I piled a bunch of stuff up in front of my door again and turned off my computer.

When I woke up, I was somehow much more tired than I had been the night before—but from what I could tell, nothing had happened. I rushed downstairs and grabbed my moonstone. For the first time in a long while no strange memories or dreams floated into focus when I touched it. Feeling slightly more in control of my life because I'd made it through a night where nothing weird had happened, I tried to embody some of the quiet confidence Anji was sure I had. But by the time Monday afternoon came around, I was feeling less sure of myself.

In English class my doubts multiplied when Velvet and Briana approached me about the auditions. "You don't actually think you stand a chance, do you, Lucia?" Velvet asked me in her nicest voice. "They want someone with power. Confidence. Someone with strong stage presence. No offense, but that's not exactly how I would describe you." She smiled at me and leaned in close, as though we were sharing a secret. "You know you're more of a behind-the-scenes girl. We've talked about this before."

I glared at her. "You've talked about it," I said, surprising myself. "I never said anything."

She smirked. "Exactly."

"You know what, Velvet?" I blurted out, my voice more of a whine than I would have liked it to be. "You don't get to decide who does and doesn't try out for the play. You're not in charge."

She rolled her eyes. "Whatever, Lucia."

I wanted to say more. Wanted to tell her I hoped she'd fall and break a leg during the audition. I wished I could tell her she had a terrible voice but had gotten so used to her dad's paid employees complimenting her her whole life that she probably thought forced compliments were real. I longed for her to know that if she did get cast, it was only because people were afraid of what her dad might do if her name wasn't on that list.

But even though I thought all of this, I knew every single one of those things was much too mean to say. As much as I wished that Velvet would someday know what it felt like to lose out on something she cared about, I knew I could never be the kind of person who would tell her that. No matter what.

Walking through the halls after school, I *still* hadn't decided for sure what I was going to do about the audition. It would be easy enough to just go home, forget about the musical, and apologize to Anji later. I knew she planned to audition with or without me. She'd be disappointed if I didn't show up, sure, but I knew she'd understand. For a moment I let myself imagine what it would feel like to get up on that stage and let everyone hear me sing. I pictured all those eyes on me and the look on Velvet's face when she realized I was someone who had a voice. That I actually could be a threat. In time, I knew, I would reclaim Will as a friend. If I also took a part in the musical away from her, it would be such sweet revenge.

But I couldn't.

Wouldn't.

Shouldn't.

I tossed my books into my backpack as quickly as I could and ran out of school before Anji got to her locker. I knew she would try to convince me to stay, and I didn't want to let her down. Even as I made my way to the side door, the one closest to my bus stop, I felt a little wriggle of doubt. Why was I running away? Hadn't I wished for the guts to do things like this? I was the one who could make that wish come true. All it would take is a little courage, and I *could* be the kind of girl who tried out for school plays. I could be the kind of girl who stood up to Velvet Mills.

The doubt about my choice was strong enough that I didn't run for the bus when I got outside. I lingered, still debating. If I left school and went home, it would be impossible to change my mind. When Daunte Adams and a few guys from the soccer team burst out of the back door near the gym, I rushed to catch the door before it closed and locked behind them. I hustled back up through the halls, toward the media center.

The library was empty today. No one had media last period, and Mrs. Davies always left right after the last bell to get her kid from preschool. I slipped inside the darkened library and found my favorite corner way in the back. I slid down to the floor, hidden among the books and the silence. I pulled my moonstone out of my pocket and rubbed the soft edges. I wished the stone would tell me what to do.

Then I realized maybe it could. *If I fell asleep,* I wondered, *what would happen?* Ever since the eclipse, every other time I'd fallen asleep with my moonstone I had acted out on some unrealized wish or thing I longed to do. If I fell asleep now and let the moonstone take charge, would I make it to the audition . . . in my dreams?

Could using the moonstone's magical power for something good really be so bad?

OUT OF THE SHADOWS

The girl stood confidently at center stage. She was one of the last to audition, and based on what she'd seen so far, she stood a good chance. With a clear voice she announced, "My name is Lucia Frank, and I'd like to audition for the role of Dorothy."

"Go ahead," the director said from somewhere in the darkened theater. "What song will you be singing?"

"'Part of Your World,' from The Little Mermaid.*"*

She heard someone snickering backstage. Then a familiar voice whispered, "As if she'll ever be part of our world. Dorothy? The Cowardly Lion, maybe . . ."

Somehow the other girl's teasing gave her strength. This was her chance to show everyone—especially herself—that she deserved this. She didn't deserve to be stuck in the shadows. She would never know how bright she could shine unless she gave herself the chance.

She knew she was perfect for the part of Dorothy, a girl who chased after her dreams to find her own happiness. Dreams, she was beginning to realize, really do come true.

Summoning courage from within, she sang her song beautifully. When she walked off the stage and into the shadowy wings, she marched past the other girl and her friends and muttered, "That was me, making things happen."

CHAPTER SIXTEEN

ucia. Lu!" I woke with a start. Anji was shaking me, whispering my name. We were in the middle of the hallway outside the theater. I took a deep breath and looked into her eyes. "Lucia!" She was squeezing my hand in her own. "Wake up." She poked my face and nudged me. "You did it," she said when my eyes finally focused on her. She held out a hand and showed me that my moonstone was resting in her open palm.

"You have my stone," I said, confused. "How did you get it?"

"I took it from you," she whispered. "I pulled it out of your pocket a few seconds ago. You looked dazed for a sec, then it was like you woke up out of some sort of half sleep."

I rubbed the moonstone's cool surface and flashes of a memory or a dream—I still didn't know what to call them exactly—flickered through my consciousness. Me, onstage, singing. "I auditioned?"

Anji closed her eyes and nodded. "Yep. I looked all over for you after school. Someone told me they saw you leaving for the bus. So when you showed up and marched out onto the stage looking not at all nervous, I got a funny feeling."

"I was going to go home," I admitted.

"But you didn't . . . ," Anji said.

"No," I said. "I guess I didn't."

"We need to talk to your mom's friend," she said. "Now. Call her."

I nodded, numb. Suze answered and invited us over for dinner. She didn't seem to think it was weird that I was calling. I guess my mom must have told her to expect to hear from me. Anji and I found Jonathan in the band room and asked him if he wanted to come along. Of course he did. I called my sister, who said she'd pick us up and drive us there.

"Where are we headed?" Romy asked as we got into the car. I gave her the address, and let her take charge. The four of us spent the whole ride over to Suze's apartment talking about everything that had happened lately. We all agreed it seemed a little silly that we were counting on Suze to give us answers—I had a feeling there was more to it than some fake dream lady could help me with. And I was so exhausted I couldn't even think straight, let alone tell her about everything that had been happening.

A few minutes later we parked and stood in front of a buzzer with four numbers. I pushed number two and waited, wondering what Suze would be like now. It had been years since I'd last seen her, and all I could remember were little snippets of a mental image from my childhood. Would she be able to help me figure my life out?

"I got us a pizza," a cheerful voice called from the other end of the intercom. "Come on up!"

"The role of dreams is—I believe—to restore a level of equilibrium in one's psyche. Dreams are often your unrealized life, bubbling up to the surface." Suze opened a white pizza box on her coffee table and handed each of us a paper plate with an American flag on it. "Sorry about the plates—Fourth of July leftovers." She gestured to the pizza in front of us and said, "Eat!"

Suze was not at all like the woman I remembered. Her bleached-blond hair had been cut into a choppy bob. She was slender and normal looking, and her apartment was crammed with campy vampire romance novels and textbooks and trinkets. Clothes were strewn across every available surface. There wasn't a crystal ball in sight, and I couldn't see traces of tarot cards or incense or any of the other things I seemed to remember her having around when I was little. These absences made me trust her a lot more.

We all grabbed a slice of pizza, but I already knew I didn't have the stomach to eat mine. Jonathan folded his slice in half, as he always did, and bit in eagerly. "Hot!" he cried, spitting a big cheesy pile onto his plate. He looked appropriately embarrassed. "Sorry. It was hot."

Anji and I sat with our slices in our lap and waited for Suze to continue telling us her dream theory. Romy stayed far off to the side, listening without eating or saying anything at all.

Suze had launched right into a monologue about sleep cycles and the subconscious the minute we walked through her front door, as though she'd been waiting years for someone to ask. I hadn't yet told her exactly why I was there, just that I'd been having especially vivid dreams. I was curious about what she had to say about dreams in a more general sense . . . maybe it would give me some easy answers about the forgotten moments, without me having to divulge too much. After all, she was my mom's friend first. I knew she'd tell Mom everything we talked about.

Suze took a big bite of her pizza and continued speaking with a full mouth. "When you dream, it's actually your unconscious acting on an underlying intention. In a sleep state, of course." As she talked, I kept thinking about how Suze wasn't anything like I'd remembered. I guess I had sort of expected her to answer the door in flowing scarves and skirts, with a cloud of incense dancing around her head. Gym clothes and pizza and flag plates felt very unnatural for someone like Suze.

"Certain dreams have different symbolism or meanings attached," she went on. "And that's what is so fascinating about the study of sleep stories. There are many hidden layers to someone's subconscious and unconscious, some of which are especially revealing."

"So what does it say about you when your dreams start to cross the line into real life?" Jonathan asked, winking at me. He wasn't exactly subtle. "Like, say you have a dream about an actual event that took place."

"A re-creation in dream state of an event you've actually experienced ?" Suze asked. "That's certainly common."

"No," Jonathan continued. "What if you dream you did something or went somewhere, and then find out that it wasn't just a dream? Like, you actually *were* there. But you thought it was just a dream."

What was he, my spokesperson?

Jonathan grinned at me, but Suze looked puzzled. She grabbed a napkin off the coffee table and dabbed at the top of her pizza slice to soak up the extra grease. "I'm not sure I'm following," Suze said, pushing the pizza box toward me. She must have noticed that I had passed my first piece to Jonathan, and I now sat there empty-handed. I wasn't hungry—only tired and paranoid. "That sounds more like déjà vu. Like, you get the feeling you've done something before?"

I had to make the conversation stop before Jonathan kept asking weird questions that were going to lead us into some strange and irrelevant territory. The fact is, I needed answers, and this was the closest I'd come to finding someone who might have some for me. "He's asking about all of this for me," I clarified. "As I mentioned on the phone, I've been having these weird dreams that I can just remember little snippets of when I wake up. But they feel very real and vivid, and are often memories of actual things that took place in the night."

Suze studied me carefully. "As in, your dreams are your reality?" She looked concerned.

"Something like that?" I said, cringing. "I've been having dreams or memories or something about places I've been and things I've done—but it turns out my actions aren't just dreams. I'm actually up and moving about, in some sort of dream *state* or something. Like I'm sleepwalking, but not."

"Are you acting like yourself during these dreamlike 'sleepwalking' incidents?" she asked.

"Not really," Jonathan said, before I had a chance to answer. "She's usually pretty shy, except when she's with us."

"She's been speaking her mind a lot more, and she went to auditions for the fall musical, and other out-of-character stuff," Anji added. "A bunch of things Lucia usually wouldn't do."

"When did this all start happening?" Suze was up and kneeling in front of her fridge, which was squeezed into her living room between the couch and a big bongo drum. It looked like she and her boyfriend used the minifridge as an end table. Clever. She grabbed a can of sparkling water and cracked it open. "Recently, I assume?"

"Just over a week ago." I was starting to get more comfortable talking about everything. I was feeling much more confident about things in general lately. Some elements of my dream persona were rubbing off on me—maybe knowing what I was capable of in my dream state made me more relaxed letting the inside bits out during the day. "I'm pretty sure everything shifted the night of the eclipse."

Suze sucked in a breath. "Do you know we used to call you Moon Child? Because you were born during an eclipse, we always felt like the moon had claimed you as one of her own. A part of her shadow, somehow."

I nodded. I did know this, of course. "Do you think the eclipse is related to any of this? Or my birthday?" I stared at Suze, willing her to give me some easy answer. Some way to make sense of everything. "And what does my moonstone have to do with it? It seems like it must be connected somehow, since all this funny stuff happens when I have it—but not when I don't."

"I'm not sure what that means." She scooted on her knees over to a little bookshelf she had in the corner of the living room. I noticed then that Suze didn't have a TV. Who doesn't have a TV? "I only know a little bit about eclipse legend. But I can't help but think all of this sounds a lot like Carl Jung's theory of the shadow." She pulled a book from a shelf and started flipping through it. "The shadow is really more of a psychological term that Carl Jung spent a lot of time studying. Basically, he believed that our shadow embodies everything in us that is repressed or denied."

"Like Jekyll and Hyde?" Jonathan asked.

"In a sense, yes." Suze was still flipping through the book but didn't seem to be finding anything particularly telling. "But Jung didn't necessarily believe that a person's shadow was completely evil, rather that there are also rejected portions of ourselves that are light. So there is a positive side of the shadow, as well as negative. Every aspect of the shadow lives in our unconscious—or so Jung thought—so we don't know what its true potential is. . . ." Suze trailed off. "I'm not a Jung scholar, but that's the gist of what I know about his shadow theory. And I can't help but feel like you're describing your shadow, Lucia. Everyone has a shadow, but only certain people have the opportunity to tap into it and realize its possibilities."

"Her *shadow*?" Romy stared at Suze, her mouth agape. "As in, Lucia's *shadow* is acting out on her behalf?"

"If that theory was accurate, then you're saying Lucia is crazy. You said this is a psychological condition, right?" I could always count on Anji to say the things I was thinking but didn't really want an answer to. "Like in *The Strange Case of Dr. Jekyll and Mr. Hyde*—I didn't finish the book, but isn't that dude nuts?"

Suze smiled. I don't know what she thought was so clever. I was more than a little freaked out here and didn't particularly appreciate her calm, dream-lady attitude at that very minute. "There are a number of scholars who believe that, yes, the shadow is just your repressed unconscious bubbling up to the surface." I didn't want any part of my insides bubbling anywhere, and I wished she wouldn't use that phrase anymore. "But—" She paused to take a sip of her fizzy water. I gritted my teeth. "I can't help but feel like there is something more to it in Lucia's case. The fact that this coincided with the eclipse, your birthday, the stone, and this all came about very suddenly? I am intrigued."

I sighed. "So what am I supposed to do?"

"I think there is someone who might have some interesting insights for us." Suze was still smiling that ridiculous, bemused smile. I didn't have the guts to tell her there was no "us" in this scenario—it was only me going crazy, so any insights should just be sent straight my way, thanks.

"If you say it's some medicine man who lives under a bridge, I'll be very amused." Jonathan looked pleased by his own humor.

"Actually, Lucia's mother is probably the best person for us to speak to."

"My mom?" I asked at the same time Romy said, "Mom?"

Suze paused, and I could sense that she was reluctant to say whatever it was she was thinking. "Your mom has always been fascinated by lunar charms, and has spent a lot of her life—particularly in the past few years—researching legends behind shadow and light. Purely as a hobby, but I know she has some interesting theories. Particularly as this relates to you." I could sense there was something more that she wasn't telling me. "I think we need to share all of this with your mom, Lucia. If you want answers, she's probably the best person to help you."

CHAPTER SEVENTEEN

Are you okay?" Romy asked me quietly on our way back toward the car. We had thought about calling my mom from Suze's house, but it was after midnight in Sweden. Suze had made me promise to call her the next day— she was certain my mom would have more to offer.

"Yeah, I'm fine." I couldn't stop thinking about everything Suze had said. The thing that scared me almost as much as anything she'd said was that I didn't necessarily *want* to figure out how to make the magic stop. I forced a smile for my sister. "Just tired."

None of us talked for a minute. I appreciated the silence. Romy walked ahead, and I looped my arm into Jonathan's and Anji's to give me something concrete to hold on to. I felt dazed and couldn't help but wonder what it took for this other side of me—my shadow?—to come out. Did I have to worry about suddenly being possessed or something by my other half while I was still technically awake? Or was it the sleep and the moonstone that activated everything? Hadn't my mom given me the stone as an amulet of protection? So why wasn't it working? I didn't have any answers, and that left me shaken and scared.

"Does anyone want to get a cupcake?" Anji proposed when we walked past a bakery. "My treat."

"In that case . . . ," Jonathan said, opening the door for us. We all walked in, and the smell of sugar was overpowering. I selected a red velvet cupcake and sat down at a small table in front of the shop window. Romy sat down next to me and wordlessly offered me a bite of her chocolate cupcake.

"So . . . Suze had some interesting thoughts," Jonathan said, finally opening up the conversation. "What do you guys think? Are you buying this whole shadow thing?"

"I don't really know what choice we have but to believe her," Anji said. She smiled at me. "It's as good a guess as any."

I licked the icing sitting in a sugary heap on top of my cupcake. "I've never really believed in all this magic theory that my mom and her friends buy into," I said finally. "But now I desperately *do* want to believe in magic, since the alternative scares the crap out of me. I want to have an answer, and to figure out how I control this thing. So yeah, I'm interested in hearing what my mom has to say. I guess I just want to know what it all means."

I stared at the wall behind Jonathan's head, certain the paisley wallpaper was moving. I really needed to sleep. "I don't necessarily love the idea that there could be some sort of shadow acting on my behalf, but I do want to know if there's something else it could be or how the shadow got out, or whatever happened. Even if my mom's theories usually sound strange, I owe it to her to bring her into this and let her try to help me." I vowed to tell Mom about the changed moonstone as soon as I could speak with her—it was time to stop denying that piece of it. Since she was the one who had given it to me, I hoped she would be able to tell me something more about how it worked.

When Romy dropped Jonathan and Anji off at their houses, they both made me promise to sleep without my moonstone again that night. But even as I stuffed the stone deep inside my backpack and hung the pack on a hook by the front door, a piece of me was yearning to keep it close for the night. I told Romy about how I felt drawn to its power. "I can't help but be curious about what else might happen if I keep it with me,"

I admitted. Most of the things I'd wished for on the night of the eclipse had come true—what more could the power of the stone offer me, if I let it take over?

As soon as I got to my room, I searched online for Carl Jung and his shadow theory. Romy read along over my shoulder. She whispered, "It isn't really any more comforting to read about than it was to have Suze tell us about it, is it?" I glanced back at her and shook my head. What we found made it seem much more like your shadow is the place where all your dark thoughts are stored. The shadow sucks them in and locks them up, holding the evil pieces of you hostage.

I quickly closed the browser and reopened a new window. A fresh search helped me find some interesting bits on doppelgangers, which seemed to be another execution of this shadow theory. A doppelganger literally meant "double walker," and a few online sites described it as a shadow-self that accompanies its owner. Back to the shadow thing again.

Doppelgangers can be evil but are also sometimes just good company for their other half—like an imaginary friend. They listen and give advice and stand behind their owner, one site said. But to me it all sounded very sketchy. Apparently it is also really bad luck if your doppelganger is seen (like, a possible indication you would soon die, so this was all just getting better by the minute), but if it does make itself visible to your family and friends, confusion abounds. That sounded familiar. I was seriously confused. I hoped my mom might be able to shed some light on things.

Soon my eyes were swimming. I longed for a good night's sleep but knew I wouldn't get one. My dad and Romy both tucked me in, and then I let myself sink into bed without fear, hoping my "shadow" wouldn't sneak out in the night. I couldn't survive another sleepless night, so I had no choice but to trust that everything would be okay with my moonstone elsewhere. As I drifted off, I thought about the auditions and wondered if I would get a callback. If I did, would I have the nerve to go through with it on my own? I really wanted to believe I could get up on that stage and prove myself worthy—without the help of sketchy magic.

After only a minute or two I fell asleep and slept dreamlessly. I woke in a fog the next morning. Nothing seemed amiss, so I hoped it had been an uneventful night. When I finally dragged myself out of the house to rush for the bus, I bumped into Will—juggling a soccer ball—at the end of his driveway. "Hey," he said with a smile.

"Hi." I was tempted to run off and avoid him like I'd done pretty much every day since I got back from Sweden. But then I remembered "I" had been spending time with him during my shadow moments. The ice between us had been broken while I thought I was sleeping, so I figured I might as well start mending things in my waking hours too. "How are you?"

"Good. I hear you auditioned for the musical?"

"I did," I said, feeling my face flush. "I decided I might as well give it a shot."

"You have a great voice. You deserve it." He kicked the ball up and caught it in his hands. "I'm sure you'll get cast—or a callback, at least."

"Yeah, well, we'll see. I don't think Velvet needs to worry about me stealing a part from her or anything."

Will looked a little uncomfortable suddenly. "Lucia . . ."

I peeked at my phone and realized I had to hustle if I was going to make the bus.

Will continued, "Velvet and I aren't really hanging out anymore. I kind of told her I didn't want to go out or whatever."

"Really?" I chewed my lip. I felt the tiniest flutter of happiness. This was the first time anyone had *ever* rejected Velvet. She got what she wanted, always. But now Will had broken up with her! Then I felt guilty for feeling happy about it. Did I really want to see her hurt? "Oh. Well, I'm sorry?"

"Don't be sorry." He laughed. "It's all good. She was kind of bossy, and I didn't really like how brutal she could be around her friends sometimes. She was pretty fun most of the time, but I guess I sort of realized we don't really have anything in common. Except you."

I shuffled my feet in the dirt and thought about what Will had said: that Velvet could be brutal to her friends. So it wasn't just me she treated badly. I guess part of me knew that, but another part of me had often wondered what I'd done wrong to make Velvet turn on me, specifically. But her cruelty had nothing to do with me and everything to do with Velvet. That's just the way she was. Last summer I had been in the wrong place, with the wrong friend, at the wrong time.

Suddenly Will's mom opened the kitchen window and yelled out, "Lucia, let me give you a ride to school. We're leaving in a few minutes."

I looked at Will. He nodded. "Okay," I yelled back. "Thanks."

"Anyway, I just thought you should know about Velvet." Will shrugged. "You want to wait for my mom up in the tree house? I'll get you a muffin. My mom made them last night."

"Yeah, totally." Will ran inside for a couple of muffins while I climbed up into the tree house. When he joined me, I asked, "So is she upset?"

"About me and her?" he asked. "I dunno. We didn't really talk about it much, so I'm not sure. I just texted her and told her we shouldn't hang out except in groups and stuff anymore."

I gaped at him. "You *texted* her? You've been going out for a couple of months. That's an eternity! Text breakups are *not* cool." I suddenly felt bad for Velvet. As mean as she'd been to me, she didn't deserve to be broken up with in a text. No one deserved that. "Seriously, Will. What's wrong with you?"

He grinned. "See? This is why it's good we're hanging out again. You can help me figure this stuff out. How was I supposed to know that?"

"Are you human?" I asked, laughing. I smacked him on the shoulder and in that simple gesture, it felt like I'd hit a reset button. For the first time in months, our friendship was creeping back to what it used to be. "Everyone knows you don't break up with someone over text. Guys are seriously weird."

"*Guys* are?" Will said, scuffing his feet on the wooden boards of the tree house. "I've seen the way Velvet acts with her friends.

I guarantee girls are a *lot* weirder than guys. Girls are impossible to understand. Some girls, anyway."

"Not me," I said. "I'm nothing like Velvet."

"You're definitely not," he said. "Thank God for that."

"Will you talk to her?" I asked. "She's probably not going to be very nice to you about it, since I'm guessing she's hurt and embarrassed. But you have to talk to Velvet face-to-face. It's the nice thing to do, and you've always been a nice guy. Promise?"

He frowned. "Really?"

"Really." I nodded. I knew Velvet well enough that I was sure she didn't handle rejection well. "You have to talk to her in person. Just tell her the truth." I couldn't believe I was advocating on behalf of my former best friend who had hurt me so badly. But if it were me in Velvet's shoes, I'd want someone to do the same. "If you don't say anything, it's going to be weird between the two of you forever. Trust me. Please?"

Will sighed. "I guess you're right." He shoved half a muffin into his mouth, slung his backpack over his shoulder, and climbed down to the ground. Through a mouthful of muffin chunks, he said, "I'll talk to Velvet, as long as you promise to ace your callback. No cold feet and no chickening out. Deal?"

"I don't even know if I'll *get* a callback," I said, climbing down the ladder after him.

"You will. So break a leg this afternoon, okay?"

I reached into my pocket for my moonstone, willing some of its strength to ooze through my skin. Squeezing it tight in my palm, I promised. "Okay."

When we got to school, there was a cluster of people gathered around the theater's double doors. Before I could make my way to the front of the pack, Anji came rushing at me. "You got a callback!" she screeched. A few people turned to look at us and Anji grinned back at all of them. "My friend Lucia, the callback queen!" she announced.

"I did?" I craned my neck to try to see over the crowd. "Did you?"

"No." She pouted briefly. But then her silver lips glimmered and turned up in a smile. "But that's okay. I didn't really expect it. I'm going to sign up to help with lighting or something so we can still be together. I'm so excited for you!"

"Did Velvet get a callback?" I asked.

Anji rolled her eyes. "Obviously."

"Well," I said, nerves churning already, even though there

was a whole day of school before the callbacks. "This should be fun."

Anji laughed. "You've got this, Lucia. Just sing like you did yesterday and you'll be fine."

We made our way toward our lockers. "Yeah, but yesterday I had the help of my stone," I said quietly. "Remember?"

"You don't need it," Anji said certainly. "It's not like the stone gives you magic powers and turns your voice into Adele's. It's still you. You just need to get up there and do your thing. Quiet confidence!"

"Easy for you to say," I muttered.

Anji bumped her hip into mine. "The audition's easy-peasy, girl. It's Velvet you need to worry about."

As if she needed to remind me.

By the end of the day I was completely exhausted again. At lunch Jonathan, Anji, and I had escaped the cafeteria and gone to the auditorium for a few extra minutes of rehearsal. In science class Anji had ignored our experiment and used most of the hour to psych me up. I spent all of English class trying to avoid Velvet, but she managed to catch me right at the end as everyone was gathering up their things. "Just give up, Lucia," she said under her breath. "So you got lucky at auditions yesterday. Now stop pretending to be someone you're not. No one's falling for your little act this past week. You'll never be me, so stop faking it."

"Knock it off," I hissed. "You can't intimidate me. And I would never *want* to be you."

Velvet smiled slowly. "Is that so?"

"I deserve a part in the play just as much as you do," I said. I felt this hatred bubbling up (there was Suze's word again). Suddenly all I wanted to do was say something horrible to Velvet. "You can't even sing—" I began, but then I stopped.

What would hurting her get me? Cutting her down, making her feel like something less, wasn't going to make me stronger. So I shook my head and said, "I shouldn't have said that. But you and I both know I *do* deserve the same shot as everyone else. Just because you think I can't do it, doesn't mean I can't. You don't even know me, so stop trying to act like you have some sort of control over my life." I released my breath a long whoosh, then stood up and left class five seconds before the bell rang.

"Lucia?" Ms. Tanner-Blank called after me. "We're not finished."

As soon as I was out in the hall, the bell rang. "We are now," I muttered. I was so done with Velvet. I thought about all the insults I could have swung at her, all the things I could have said to shake her confidence before the callbacks.

Waves of people pushed at me from all sides, and I was suddenly overcome with another rush of extreme exhaustion. I felt for the moonstone in my pocket. When I did, fatigue swept over me again. I stumbled and someone lifted me up by my elbow. An unfamiliar voice said, "You okay?"

In a haze, I shook my head but couldn't get any words to come. I wasn't sure how much longer I could keep myself up. I felt like I was inside a fishbowl—sounds were muffled, and everything seemed to be swimming around me as if the whole school had been flooded with water. I rubbed my eyes, but they just clouded over more. I felt like I was going to be sick.

Stumbling again, I dragged myself toward the girls' bathroom at the end of the hallway. I could hear laughter nearby, and the sounds of voices echoed around me like we were in an enormous cave. Clutching at my stone for strength, I tripped through the door of the bathroom and collapsed in an empty stall.

As my mind slid further and further out of my control,

I tried to rouse myself. I had to stop myself from falling asleep. What was happening to me? It was time for callbacks. My cheek pressed against the wall in the stall, and I felt a wave of nausea rush over me. My face was flattened against the stall door, my hands on my knees. I knew it was disgusting and germ filled and I wanted to heave, but I couldn't make myself get back up. Fighting against the nausea and extreme exhaustion, I mustered up the strength to press my foot against the toilet so I wouldn't accidentally fall into it.

Not this time, I thought, begging and pleading with myself. *You can do this callback on your own.* But the thought was miles away, like my real life was a dream and something was trying to pull me out of it. *Wake up!* I pleaded with myself. *Wake up and show Velvet she was wrong about you.*

OUT OF THE SHADOWS

Rushing through the emptying hallways, the girl had one thing on her mind: revenge. It was the only way to get her last wish. "Hey," she called out, trying to catch her former best friend's attention. "Can we talk?"

The other girl spun around, bobbed black hair swishing against her chin. She snipped, "What is there to talk about? Are you here to wish me luck? Beg me to put in a good word for you? Dream on."

"Here's what I'm wondering: Why are you bothering to audition? Have you ever realized that the only people who compliment your singing voice are people on your dad's staff?" The girl smiled coldly, keeping her voice level. "You can't sing."

The other girl's mouth opened slightly. "What?"

"But the bigger question is, will your parents even come and see you if you do get a part? You're the one who told me they never wanted a kid in the first place. Did you think maybe getting a part in the fall musical would trick them into thinking you're worth their time and pride? It's not enough, Velvet." She put her face up close to the other girl's and whispered, "I know Will dumped you. Your parents don't have time for you. I don't need you anymore. Have you ever considered the fact that anyone who really gets to

know you figures out you're not a good person? We all walk away when we realize the truth. Eventually, you won't have anyone left."

She shrugged as the other girl's tears came. "But if you think getting a part in the play will somehow make you more loved, then good luck at your callback, Velvet. I'm sure you'll do great."

CHAPTER EIGHTEEN

When Anji and Jonathan woke me a short while later, I immediately felt for the warm stone in my pocket. It wasn't there. When Anji saw I was looking for it, she dropped it into my hand. "Here," she said. "Is that what you're looking for?"

As soon as I rubbed my fingers across the stone's smooth surface, everything rushed back to me in a flood of interconnected images. What I'd said to Velvet, my performance, the elation I had felt when I knew I'd sung better than anyone else at the callbacks. I studied my friends' expressions. I didn't even need to ask them what had happened. I already knew.

Anji chewed the corner of her lip. "You did great onstage. There are still a few people left to audition, but right now your chances look pretty good."

Jonathan nodded, but he looked worried.

I hung my head. I felt no joy about the audition. Instead, I was sickened by what I'd said to Velvet. The deepest, shadowiest thoughts inside my head had come crawling out. I knew I had said things that poked at every nook and cranny of her vulnerability—and for what? Was stooping to my former best friend's level of mean what it would take for me to feel like I'd gotten payback for her hurting me? Is this the way I wanted to stand up to her?

I told my friends about what I remembered from touching the stone, and how I'd said some hurtful things to Velvet before the auditions. "I didn't mean to fall asleep. I can't believe I said what I think I said!"

"What did you say?" Anji asked, holding my locker open for me while I gathered my stuff. "Do you remember the specifics?"

I shook my head. "I can't tell you," I said. I knew it wasn't fair for me to air Velvet's insecurities in front of Anji or Jonathan. Saying all those things to Velvet in private was horrible enough, but telling someone else all of her greatest fears was worse. This wasn't about keeping secrets from my friends—it was about keeping someone else's secrets a secret. "I just said a bunch of stuff I know she's always been worried about. I shouldn't have. I feel awful." I glanced at them. "How'd she do in her audition?"

"She hasn't gone yet," Anji said, pushing her glittery pink lips out in a pout. "She's singing second to last. But I saw her going into the bathroom a while ago. Now that I think about it, I don't think she ever came back to the theater."

"Which bathroom?" I asked, worried I'd said enough to crush her confidence.

"The weird one by the band room," Anji told me. "The one with the broken sink."

"Wait here, okay? I'll be back in a sec." Leaving my friends at my locker, I hurried down the hall. I knew I had to make things right with Velvet. Hurting her in such a flat-out-mean way, jeopardizing her audition—that wasn't the kind of person I wanted to be. I had to try to fix it. She'd done plenty of mean things to me, but I wasn't the kind of person who needed an eye for an eye. Making her hurt wouldn't take away any of the pain I'd felt. I rushed into the bathroom. Velvet was washing her face in the leaky sink, and when she looked up at me, it was obvious she had been crying. "Velvet . . . ," I said, stepping toward her.

"What do you want now?" she said, her voice shaky. "You

got what you wanted. I bailed on my audition. I don't even want a part, so I figured I should just let you have it. You won this round, Lucia. Bravo."

"I'm so, so sorry," I said. "I shouldn't have said what I did. It was really mean. I wasn't trying to *win*, I was just . . ." I trailed off. There was no excuse for what I'd said.

"It's all true, and you know it," Velvet said, lifting her chin defiantly. "It's not like you said anything I don't already know. Whatever." She clenched her teeth and tried to smile. I knew it was a false front, but Velvet prided herself on looking cool. She wouldn't let anyone see her sweat, not if she could help it. "I have too much going on anyway. I don't need to be in the stupid musical."

"The stuff I said, it wasn't all true," I told her, trying again to apologize.

"Can you just shut up?" she said. "Don't act like you feel sorry for me. I know my parents don't hate me. And at least they're not divorced, like yours. Why don't you focus on your own issues for once? As for Will? Who cares if things didn't work out—he's a jerk if he doesn't want me. It's his loss. And guess what? *Our* friendship ended because I wanted it to. I moved on. I'm fine, okay, Lucia?"

"Velvet," I began. I knew she was just acting tough. I wanted to find some way to comfort her, to make her feel better, to get her to not hate me. "I just—"

Velvet groaned. "Shut. Up. Stop talking, please. We're not friends anymore, Lucia. Don't act like you know me. You don't know anything." She wiped her face with a wet paper towel one last time. Then she balled the rough paper up and threw it in the trash. She made her way toward the door, and then turned back. "Do you need me to tell you I'm not mad at you? Will that make you feel better? I know how you are about arguments—sensitive, shy Lucia doesn't like people to be upset with her." She rolled her eyes. "Words might hurt you, but they don't hurt me. I'm fine. Seriously."

"What I said was mean, Velvet," I said again. "I just hope you'll forgive me."

"If you need me to tell you I forgive you, fine. I forgive you. I really do." She tilted her head and looked at me with something like a smile on her face. "But I will say I have just slightly more respect for you now that I know you have a backbone."

"I want you to go to your callback," I blurted out. "I don't want to be the reason you don't get a part."

"You're giving yourself *way* too much credit," she said,

laughing in an unconvincing way. "As if I'd be scared away by your little rant. Fine. If it's going to make you feel better after what you said, then I'll go out and sing." She narrowed her eyes. "Consider us even. For everything."

"Break a leg," I said quietly as she walked toward the door.

"Whatever," she shot back.

When I got back to my locker, Anji and Jonathan were chatting quietly together. "Let's go," I said, throwing the rest of my stuff into my bag.

"Feel better?" Anji asked.

"Not really," I said honestly.

Jonathan cleared his throat. "So, just out of curiosity . . . did you ever consider leaving your moonstone home today?"

"Yeah, I considered it." I grabbed my bag and angrily slammed my locker closed. "But then I didn't."

"Nope, you didn't," Jonathan agreed. "Think it's time to finally admit that the stone is the problem?"

I took a deep breath. "Yeah. Especially since it seems like it's getting more powerful. Or maybe I'm getting better at reading it or something? When you guys woke me up a little bit ago and I touched the stone, the whole afternoon flashed through my head like a movie on fast-forward. I remember everything pretty clearly." I paused and looked at them. "When all of this first started happening, I would only see little snippets of what I'd done or said when I woke up. I don't really get why I'm able to remember more now."

"Have you called your mom yet?" Anji asked.

"No. I will this afternoon. I didn't have time before school."

"Want us to come home with you for moral support?" Jonathan offered.

I gratefully accepted, and we headed for the front door. I hoped they were okay with taking the bus to my house. "The other thing that happened today . . . ," I began, then wondered if I should admit to them that it almost felt like the stone had taken over for a while after class. If I told them, I knew they would force me to get rid of the moonstone right away, and I wasn't sure I was willing to do that. But what had happened after school—when it felt like I was being dragged underwater—was scary. In the last few days it seemed like the line between awake and asleep was beginning to blur. Today it had almost felt as if my shadow was determined to take over. I'd been unable to keep myself awake, and that was terrifying.

"Lucia? *What* else happened today?" Anji prompted.

"Nothing," I said, shrugging. "It was nothing."

As soon as we stepped outside, a car horn honked. The car was unfamiliar, so at first I ignored it, even though we were the only kids standing outside the school's front doors. Then a familiar figure got out of the driver's seat and rushed toward me.

"Mom?" I gasped. I let her sweep me up in a hug. I hadn't realized how much I'd missed those hugs. "What are you doing here?"

"My flight landed a couple hours ago," she said. "I rented a car in Newark and drove straight here. Your dad said you were staying late today. For an audition?" She looked at me strangely. "Lucia! Your hair . . . it's purple. What else have I missed?"

"Yep, purple," I said, laughing. "It's cute, huh? And yeah, I had a callback for *The Wizard of Oz*. I can tell you about that later—what are you doing here?" I introduced Jonathan and Anji, who looked as confused as I felt.

"As soon as I got your e-mail this weekend, I knew we had to talk face-to-face. I feel like we just can't connect over Skype. You're my daughter, and I want to make things right between us," she said in her gushy way. "I was trying to figure out when to come, and then your sister called yesterday morning. She told me she thought I should come as soon as I could. She wouldn't tell me anything, but considering the fact that Romy hasn't willingly called me in months, I figured I should take her request for help seriously."

"Romy called you?" I asked, surprised.

"She did. She's worried about you, and told me I was needed. I live far, but not so far that I can't get here quickly when I need to be with you. While I was on my layover in Stockholm last night, I got an e-mail from Suze telling me you'd been to see her." She glanced at Jonathan and Anji. "Are these the friends who went with you to talk to her?"

I nodded. "What did Suze tell you?"

"Not a lot," she said. "But she said you'd have some questions. Let's go home. We can talk there." She opened the passenger door for me.

I turned back to my friends. "Will you come along?"

Anji opened the back door without hesitation. "If you need us, we're in."

We got home, and Mom rustled through the fridge to find us a snack. She clucked at the pickings, groaning when she found a container of non-organic yogurt. "Not your house anymore, Mom," I said, a warning note in my voice. "You left and lost the right to comment."

"You're right." She sighed. She opened the pantry and pulled out a bag of chips. "Go for it. I'll cut up some veggies later."

Jonathan and Anji and I ate chips while I filled my mom in on everything that had happened to me over the past week and a half. I told her about the eclipse, and my wishes, the missing nights, my sick day, and the auditions. By the time I told her about what had happened that afternoon, even my mom had started chowing down on chips.

"This is not how it was supposed to work," Mom said once I was done. She shook her head slowly.

"Not how *what* was supposed to work?" I asked.

Mom spoke quietly, as if to herself, "Your Shadow Half was supposed to be scared off by the stone."

"My Shadow Half? Is this the same thing as that Carl Jung guy's shadow stuff Suze was talking about?"

"Sweetheart," my mom said, leaning across the counter to take my face in her hand. "You know you were born during a lunar eclipse."

I nodded and said sarcastically, "You've mentioned it once or a thousand times. I'm pretty aware of that fact."

"You also know I've been studying stories and secrets of the moon my whole life. Quite honestly, I couldn't believe it when you were born during a magical event. It's a blessing to be born during such a charmed time. You're my Moon Child."

"Yeah, Mom, I know that, too. But what on earth is my Shadow Half?" I glanced at Anji and Jonathan, trying to gauge their reactions. They both smiled back at me encouragingly. "Is it some sort of technical, official name for why I'm going crazy? Is this something that's happened to other people? What is going on?"

"Everyone born during an eclipse is technically a child of the moon's shadow," Mom said. The front door opened then, and my sister appeared in the front hall. After a short, somewhat chilly greeting for my mom—Romy did, at least, give Mom a small hug—my sister joined us in the kitchen to hear the rest of the story. My mom went on. "Because you were born in that rare time when a shadow stretches between the earth and the moon, there is a legend that says a small piece of *your* shadow was trapped within the eclipsed moon when you were born."

I nodded but had a hard time believing this. It sounded like more of my mom's mumbo jumbo. "Is it trapped forever?" I felt like I probably already knew the answer, given that my "Shadow Half" had apparently been out and about, taking nighttime strolls without my permission. But I knew I had to ask to be sure.

"No, not forever. This particular legend says that after the day of your birth, the next time your body is exposed to a total lunar eclipse—one that isn't hidden by clouds or in the wrong part of the world for you to experience its full effect—this piece of your shadow escapes back into your body and takes over for a time. The Shadow Half is born again during a lunar eclipse."

I widened my eyes, not totally understanding. I said the only thing I could think of: "That's seriously creepy."

"It is," my mom admitted. "But since I knew about this legend and knew there was a small chance you'd be born during the eclipse, I was obviously eager to protect you if in fact your birth did take place during the celestial event. As you can imagine, I didn't want a fractured piece of your shadow escaping *at all* later in life. It sounded dangerous, so I found a way to protect you. I procured a moonstone that I was told would reflect your shadow during an eclipse. Your Shadow Half would be frightened away by the moonstone's light properties."

"Huh," Anji muttered. "So what you're saying is, if you *didn't* have a moonstone and you were born during an eclipse, you'd be eclipsed by your own shadow? That is seriously messed up." Surely my friends thought my mom was a total wacko now. I didn't really disagree.

"It seems that I was wrong," Mom said seriously. "The moonstone doesn't appear to have offered the protection I was seeking."

Jonathan said, "Can you get your money back? Seems to me, whoever sold you that thing has a real racket going on."

My mom laughed, and I smiled gratefully at Jonathan. Things had gotten a little too serious for my taste. Shadows, eclipses, protective stones . . . it was all very disturbing.

"Can I see the moonstone?" Mom asked.

I pulled it out of my pocket and handed it over. She sucked in a breath and said, "It changed."

"Yeah," I said. "That dark streak appeared sometime during the night of the eclipse. Why?"

Mom shook her head sadly. "I don't know."

After a pause, where we all just stared at the innocent-looking stone, Jonathan cleared his throat. "Think there's any chance the stone might have sucked up Lucia's shadow? Maybe it's hanging out in there? That could be the black stuff. . . ."

Anji leaned forward to look past me at Jonathan. "Like, instead of reflecting it away like it was supposed to do, the moonstone *caught* her shadow during the eclipse? So maybe Lucia's been carrying her own Shadow Half around in her pocket all this time."

"That would explain why the weird stuff only happens when she has the moonstone." Jonathan shrugged.

Romy and I exchanged a look. "Is that possible?" I asked my mom.

She frowned. "Anything's possible. This isn't an exact science, so there are never guarantees about how it will work. It's all based on legend. With this kind of magic, you just sort of guess and then hope for the best."

"You didn't know how it would work, exactly?" I blurted. "You gave me a stone that would supposedly protect me, but instead it let some sort of creepy shadow come hang out with me when I was sleeping?"

"There are no guarantees in life, Lucia. You can't plan everything—sometimes things happen for a reason, and you just have to go with it," my mom said, and I knew she was talking about more than my stone. "Anyway, it's not a 'creepy' shadow . . . it's a piece of *your* shadow. No matter what happened on your birthday, it's very clear this is your Shadow Half that's acting out. From what you've told me about how your birthday wishes have begun to come true, it does seem that there's a piece of you inside that stone. Your shadow is acting out on some of your repressed desires when you allow it to."

I thought about what I'd said to Velvet today. Sure, I'd thought some of those things about her, but only in the private, hidden spaces of my mind. What else was my Shadow Half capable of? What more would it say, if I let it? What other things might it get up to? "So what do I do?" I asked, looking from my friends, to my sister, and back to my mom.

"Ultimately," my mom said slowly, "that's going to be up to you. But it does seem that Jonathan may be on the right track. I suspect that if you get rid of the moonstone, the loose piece of your shadow will be gone too."

I nodded, knowing she was probably right. Yet something in the deepest, darkest corners of my mind pushed the seed of a question forward, until it wedged itself up under the edge of my skull and knocked for attention: *If I give up my moonstone, does that mean everything will go back to the way it used to be?*

I wasn't sure I wanted that.

CHAPTER NINETEEN

The Wizard of Oz cast list was going to be posted before school on Wednesday morning. Part of me couldn't wait to see the list, but another part of me was terrified. I felt a little like I'd cheated at the auditions, and I wondered what would happen if I actually got a part. Would I have the courage to stand onstage and rehearse, or would I be forced to let my moonstone take over?

I slept without the stone near me again on Tuesday night. After everything I'd learned in the past few days—as well as what my own instincts were telling me—I wanted to take some time to figure out what I was going to do before letting myself near it again. I was probably imagining it, but as I drifted off to sleep that night, I could almost feel it calling to me from downstairs—as though my Shadow Half yearned to get out again, and all I needed was to hold the stone and let it take over.

My mom dropped me off at school, just like she had every day throughout elementary school. I yawned as I walked into the building. She and I had stayed up, talking for hours the night before. As soon as Dad had gotten home from work, my mom filled him in on everything that was going on. Afterward, my whole family ate dinner together, and it was a lot less awkward than I had expected it to be. My parents laughed together, even, and I was relieved that they were the kind of divorced parents who could still stand to be around each other. After we cleaned up, my dad and Romy gave Mom and me time alone so we could talk. Apparently my sister had gotten all of her own issues off her chest months ago, so she left me alone to vent. Romy told me she didn't need to rehash anything with Mom again—she just needed time to get over everything and figure out how to rebuild their relationship.

We sat together on my bed, and Mom told me she and Dad had been drifting apart for years. Even though my dad was more reluctant to admit it, she knew they were stifling a piece of themselves by staying together. It was nice to hear her admit she felt like she'd made a mistake by moving to Sweden. It was a rash decision, she said, but it had seemed logical at the time.

Now that she'd had more time to miss us, she confessed that she should have thought her plan through more carefully. I told her that it felt like she had simply disappeared from our lives when we needed her most. She promised she would speak with Johanna about possibly moving nearer to us until Romy and I graduated from high school. Mom had been wooed by the promise of a whole new life in a new place with a new identity, it seemed, and now she was missing the pieces she'd left behind when she went after it.

Though it was difficult, I forced myself to be honest through our whole conversation. Even though I still didn't understand some of Mom's decisions, I felt like we were finally in a place where we could talk about things as they came up. Maybe, someday, I'd come to accept why she'd done everything the way she had, but for now I at least felt like I was being heard. Mom was going to stick around for a week or so before she went back to Sweden to talk to Johanna and figure everything out, and for that I was grateful. I liked having her back in my daily life, and it was comforting smelling her "relax" tea in person again.

After Mom dropped me off at school, I weaved through the jam-packed Hudson Middle School halls to get to the auditorium. Just like the day before, a crowd milled around the theater doors. Anji was nowhere to be seen, so I pressed into the back of the group and craned my neck for a view of the cast list. For a brief moment I spotted my name—but then someone's head moved so I couldn't see what part I'd gotten. But I'd gotten a part!

"Proud?" Velvet said, sidling up beside me.

I tried again to look at the list. There I was . . . *Dorothy*!

I gulped. Then I checked again. There was no mistaking it—I had somehow gotten the lead in the fall musical. A few people turned and congratulated me, and I felt like I was living someone else's life. But it wasn't—this was *my* life.

I looked at Velvet, then back at the list. A quick scan told me Velvet had been cast as Munchkin/Ensemble, alongside her friend Mariah. Briana had been cast as the Wicked Witch of the West. I saw Briana's face fall when she looked at the list and realized she'd gotten a better part than Velvet's. Velvet glared at her so-called best friend, not even offering her congratulations. Briana apologized while Velvet crossed her arms and glowered.

Getting cast as a Munchkin was better than nothing, but I knew Velvet probably wouldn't see it that way. I had a feeling she'd see this as failure. "Congrats on making the cast, Velvet," I said, reaching out to touch her arm. "Listen, I'm—" Once again I began to apologize for what had happened yesterday, to tell her how much I regretted what had been said.

But before I could say anything, Anji ran up. She looked at my face and broke into a huge smile. "You got in?" She jumped up and down, then turned to study the list. She screeched, "Dorothy? No way! Lucia, you're *Dorothy*!"

Jonathan came up behind us. He, too, looked at the list and whooped. He pumped his arm in the air and hollered, "Yes!"

Velvet stepped forward, glaring at my friends. "You know *you* didn't get a part, right?" She looked at Anji. "*You* didn't even get a callback." She turned to Jonathan and said, "And you didn't try out. You're acting like you got cast, and really, you're just wannabes."

"Excuse me?" Anji said, stepping forward. I felt squeezed between them and found it hard to catch my breath.

"Seriously . . . why are you so excited?" Velvet flapped her hands in the air and pretended to scream the way Anji had. "Do you see your name on that list? No?" She muttered, "Freaks."

Jonathan's hands were balled into fists at his side. His face turned red, and he stepped backward just a hair.

"I feel bad for all of you." Velvet shook her head sadly. She looked at Anji and Jonathan, and said, "Obviously Lucia had to find *someone* to be friends with after everything that happened between us . . ." She turned to me and smiled. "But I didn't realize you'd pick such losers. I guess you take what you can get when you're desperate."

I opened my mouth to speak up, to tell her she was wrong, but found myself speechless. I reached into my pocket, looking for my moonstone. I couldn't feel its smooth edges, the coolness of the stone. I pushed my hand farther into my pocket, convinced it must be hidden in a fold of fabric. But then I remembered it wasn't. I'd left it at home that morning, and suddenly I hated myself for making such a foolish decision.

I felt the same rush of panic I had on the night of the eclipse. I needed the moonstone. Now more than ever I felt sure I could use its strength and protection. The courageous power of my shadow nestled inside the moonstone would help me stand up to Velvet in the way I needed to, to tell her she was wrong, to defend my friends. I knew that if I were able to float away and let my Shadow Half take over, it would help me. It would allow me to say all the things I had been afraid to say.

A moment passed, then another. It felt like time was standing still while Velvet smirked at all of us. Her words echoed around me in the emptying hall: *Desperate. Freaks. Losers.*

Suddenly I felt something bubble up within me. I *could* say the things I wanted to without the moonstone or its magic. I didn't need the stone or my shadow—all the same thoughts and feelings and courage were inside me, too. My mouth opened and words spilled out: "They're excited for *me*, Velvet. No, neither of them got a part in the musical, but they're happy for me anyway. That's what makes both of them such great friends. They're celebrating my success. I wish you would try it sometime."

Velvet glared at me, but it had no effect. I refused to be scared of her anymore.

"And don't even *try* to suggest that I'm only friends with Anji and Jonathan because I'm desperate. I can't believe how lucky I am to have found them. Because they've helped me understand what it means to be a friend—someone who doesn't judge, doesn't shame, doesn't make me feel less worthy just so they can feel better about themselves. I'm only sorry I didn't realize a long time ago that friendship is *not* what you and I had." I linked arms with Jonathan and Anji. "I hope someday you can figure out what it means too, because it's the best thing in the world. I really am very sorry I said what I did to you yesterday—it wasn't fair or kind, and I hope you can forgive me for being intentionally mean. But if you don't?" I took a deep breath and nodded. "Well, I'll survive."

Velvet gaped at me. I turned and tugged my friends down the hall.

"That was amazing," Anji said with a huge grin. "That took guts."

"Gaaah!" I released a pent-up sigh. "*Now* I feel better."

"No moonstone?" Jonathan asked, tilting his head.

"Nope." I squeezed each of their arms more tightly. "I'm done with it. From now on, it's only me." I grinned. "*All* me."

That afternoon my friends joined me on my walk to the river. I felt light as we made our way down the sidewalk. Kicking up piles of leaves, we sang as loud as we could, not caring who heard.

At the river, though, we all grew silent. As we stood looking out over the swimming hole below, I couldn't help but think of all the times I'd stood in this same spot with Will, ready to jump; remembered that breathless, uncertain feeling as I soared through open air, hoping for a safe landing.

"I feel like we're at a funeral," Jonathan said somberly. "Here lies Lucia's shadow. May you rest in pieces?"

"Is that what this is like, then?" Anji asked. "Like we're killing your shadow if you get rid of it?"

"We're not *killing* it," I said, laughing. "We're just keeping this escaped Shadow Half from taking over. If my mom's right, it was only a sliver of my shadow that got trapped in the moon on the night I was born. That little piece is now stuck in the moonstone, but there's still a piece of my shadow left in me. And I can use that fragment how and when I want. On *my* terms."

The stone felt warm in my palm. I gave it a squeeze and, for just a moment, wondered if I was making the right choice. But I knew I had the support of my friends and family to help keep me afloat, no matter what happened next. So before the moonstone could pull me back in, I tossed it over the side of the bridge and watched it plummet into the clear, frothing water below.

It was gone. But it had left a piece of its magic behind.

Even if Will and I might not ever be friends exactly the way we used to be, at least we were *something* again—and I was feeling pretty sure things would continue to get better from here.

I knew my relationship with my mom had changed forever too, but by finally being honest with her, we could begin to heal the wounds left from the divorce and her moving away.

Maybe I wouldn't ever be the kind of girl who *loves* the spotlight, but at least now I finally knew how good it felt to go after the things I wanted and to give myself a chance to shine.

And while I was sure my friendship with Velvet would never go back to the way it had once been, I vowed to make sure she knew I would always be there for her if she ever needed me as a friend again.

Before the eclipse I never would have guessed how much fun it could be to suddenly feel so unlike myself. But on the night of my thirteenth birthday, tucked inside a fold between the moon and the earth, everything changed.

I knew things were going to be better for me from now on. The moonstone was gone, but the new me was here to stay.

ACKNOWLEDGMENTS

Lucia's story has been in the works for almost a decade, and so many people have helped me with the plot, structure, magic issues, and characterization that it's almost impossible to put together a comprehensive thank-you list. If I've inadvertently left anyone off, I'll blame the oversight on my moonstone.

First, thanks to pals Catherine Clark, Anica Rissi, Robin Wasserman, Sarah Mlynowski, Jennifer Echols, Barb Soderberg, and Melissa Waskiewicz (along with Chloe and Zoe) for your detailed, expert editorial notes and conversations about this story at various stages of the book's development.

A million thanks to my team of junior editors—Eva Breiland, Krittika Prajapati, Sophia Caputo, Charlotte Iannone, Molly Trischitta, Alexa Nogler, Milla Downing, Henry Downing, Ruby Downing, Aidan Roy, Emily Sather, Sasha Orr, and Caroline Claeson—who helped immensely in the final months of revision. You all amazed me with your thoughtful suggestions and comments. I hope I have the opportunity to work with some of you again, years from now, when you're getting paid to do this job! Also, thanks to my junior editors' parents and teachers—*especially* Jason Lewis and Lynn Flynn—who helped to cultivate book lovers and eagerly connected me with some of these brilliant, enthusiastic readers.

Hugs and thanks to my editor at Aladdin, Fiona Simpson, for believing in this story and helping me find the right magic to make it shine. Also thanks to the rest of the Simon & Schuster crew for your support over the years, especially Mara Anastas, Katherine Devendorf, Julie Doebler, Jessica Handelman, Tricia Lin, and the incredible sales and marketing team. I'm also enormously grateful to have my dapper agent, Michael Bourret, by my side—he has cheerfully read, commented, and made brilliant suggestions on various versions of this book at least a dozen times. Thanks also to Ari Lewin, who helped me shape the seed of an idea into book form so very long ago (and suggested the addition of a moonstone!).

There is nothing better than seeing a book's cover for the first time and being able to cheer, "YES! That is exactly what I wanted." Huge thanks to artist Julia Blattman, who created the gorgeous, whimsical art that graces the jacket of this book.

There are three novels—by three of my favorite authors— that were published while I was writing this story that motivated me to keep going when I was very tempted to give up. Thanks to Victoria Jamieson (*Roller Girl*), Kate Messner (*All the Answers*), and Natalie Lloyd (*A Snicker of Magic*) for writing beautiful, inspiring books that kept me chugging along. These three stories deserve space on every reader's bookshelf!

The strangest thing happened one day while I was rewriting the first half of this novel. My Pandora station introduced me to Brett Dennen's "Just Like the Moon," and when I heard the opening lines of the song—*I believe that you were born during an eclipse / and the stars named you moon child*—it felt like a sign that *Moon Shadow* was finally on the right track. (Yes, I borrowed Lucia's nickname, "Moon Child," from the song—thanks, Brett!)

Cheers to the Nerdy Book Club, who have welcomed me with a big, bookish hug, and to all the teachers who have invited me into your classrooms live and via Skype over the past few years. You and your students inspire me to keep writing stories!

I am enormously grateful to the Minnesota State Arts Board, who awarded me an Artist Initiative Grant that helped me carve out time to finish rewriting this story. It was just the nudge and support I needed at exactly the right time. I am proud to live in a state that supports artists in such a meaningful way.

Finally, thanks to my very loving and supportive family

ACKNOWLEDGMENTS

(especially Greg, Milla, Henry, and Ruby), a crew of great friends, various baristas, incredible neighbors, and my snuggly dog . . . you have all listened to me talk about this story way too much. Woo-hoo! It's finally done!

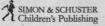

ADVENTURE TAKES FLIGHT!

"A WINNING MIX OF MODERN
ADVENTURE AND CLASSIC FANTASY."

—Rick Riordan, author of the Percy Jackson & the Olympians series